201  W9-CGO-877

DATE DUE

DOUBLE CROSS

A Chloe & Levesque
MYSTERY

BOOK 2

Norah McClintock

Kane Miller
A DIVISION OF EDC PUBLISHING

McLean County Unit #5
201-EJHS

The Chloe and Levesque Series

Over the Edge
Double Cross

First American Edition 2010
Kane Miller, A Division of EDC Publishing

Double Cross. Copyright © 2000 by Norah McClintock.
All rights reserved. First published by Scholastic Canada Ltd.

All rights reserved.

For information contact:
Kane Miller, A Division of EDC Publishing
PO Box 470663
Tulsa, OK 74147-0663
www.kanemiller.com
www.edcpub.com

Library of Congress Control Number: 2009942494

Printed and bound in the United States of America
1 2 3 4 5 6 7 8 9 10
ISBN: 978-1-935279-68-6

To Spuddy and Brulie
and good old Ward Cleaver

Chapter 1

All I did was scout out the one remaining free seat in the school cafeteria. Since when is that a crime? All I said — and I said it nicely — was, "Excuse me, but is this seat taken?"

He — a guy I had never seen before — scowled at me as if I were a cockroach that had taken on human form. Then he said — well, let's just say he came close to making me blush, which isn't easy. I'm a city kid. I know how to insult with the best of them. Who would have thought some high school kid in piddly little middle-of-nowhere East Hastings could shock me?

I don't know about you, but when I innocently lob a question at someone and that person responds by smashing an insult back at me, I do one of two things. I either ignore that person — Levesque calls it taking the high road — or I get right back in his face. This time, I did the latter. I yanked out the empty chair across from the guy and sat down. And while I was pulling my sandwich and my apple out of my lunch bag, I said, "I'm a big believer in first impressions, and my first impression of you is that you're someone I don't want to get to know any better. But I don't want to eat standing up, either, and this is a public place."

The guy, who, annoyingly, was kind of cute, glowered at me. He looked like he was aching to say something nasty, but since he had already fired the deadliest weapon in his arsenal and it hadn't blown me away, he seemed at a loss for words. Instead, he got up and started out of the cafeteria, leaving the remains of his nutritionally unbalanced lunch (I can't help it, I notice these things) on the table in front of me. I looked at the mess of gravy-soaked french fries and the half-eaten burger on his abandoned tray. If he thought I was going to clean up his mess . . .

"Hey!" I yelled.

A lot of people turned to look at me. He didn't.

"Hey, you," I yelled. "You in the jean jacket!"

He stopped. He turned slowly.

"You forgot something," I said, good and loud, so everyone in the place could hear me. "Didn't your mother teach you to clean up after yourself?"

His cobalt-blue eyes cut into me like lasers. He strode back to the table where I was sitting, scooped up the lunch tray, and dumped the whole mess into my lap. Then he stormed out of the room.

For a moment, the cafeteria was silent. Then a buzz started. Partly I felt foolish. Mostly I felt angry. I got up, grabbed a handful of paper napkins from a dispenser in the middle of the room, and started to clean up as best I could.

"That was a gutsy move," said Lena Joice at the next table. Lena sits at the very front of my chemistry class.

"Who is that guy, anyway?" I asked.

"Jonah Shackleton."

"What's his problem, apart from the fact that he's a pig?"

She shrugged. "It's the first Monday of the month."

Call me stupid, but, "Huh?"

"Visiting day is the first Sunday of the month. So on the first Monday of the month, Shackleton's a wild animal in a bad mood. The rest of the time, he's just a wild animal."

"Visiting day?"

"At the prison."

This resulted in another not-too-intelligent look from me.

"Shackleton's dad is serving twenty-five to life," Lena said. "He murdered Shackleton's mother."

Great. The guy's mother had been murdered, and what had I said to him? Didn't your mother teach you to clean up after yourself?

"He pushed her down the basement stairs five years ago," Lena said. "She landed on the concrete floor and broke her neck. I'm surprised you didn't know."

"How would I know? I wasn't living here five years ago." In fact, I had been in East Hastings for a grand total of five months . . . and counting.

"You're living in his house," Lena said.

His house? No one had said anything to me about living in a house where a murder had been committed.

* * *

That afternoon I walked home from school with Ross Jenkins. That's walked with as in walked

3

alongside of, not as in a boyfriend-girlfriend thing. Ross is a year older than me, so he isn't in any of my classes. But he's editor of the school newspaper and I work on the paper. We had gotten to know each other because of that and I guess you could say we were friends. We hung a left at the police station where my stepfather Levesque works — he's the chief of police in East Hastings — and were heading past the hardware store, when, "Hey, it's that guy!" I said.

Jonah Shackleton was walking up and down in front of the East Hastings Municipal Building, carrying a big sign. I didn't have to strain much to read the big black letters on either side: FREE HAROLD SHACKLETON. HAROLD SHACKLETON IS INNOCENT.

"I heard he was back," Ross said, in a tone that surprised me. Ross is a nice guy, very friendly, always curious about what makes people tick. He likes to tell stories about the local characters and their idiosyncrasies. But he didn't sound curious or even friendly when he talked about Jonah Shackleton. He sounded like he had made up his mind about Jonah, and what he had decided wasn't good. "Looks like he's changed his tactics and gone low-tech."

"What are you talking about, Ross?"

"Shackleton was using the school computers to mount a Free Harold Shackleton e-mail campaign. He was saying that the East Hastings police department railroaded an innocent man. Now he's not allowed to use school computers without supervision. I guess that's why he's making a fool of himself

4

by walking around in public like that." He took my elbow and steered me across the street. When we drew parallel with Jonah Shackleton, Ross didn't even glance at him.

"What's the story with him?" I asked.

He snorted.

It was just a guess, but, "You don't like him, do you?"

"He put me in the hospital. Broke my jaw. I had to have it wired shut."

I stared at Ross, who, like I say, is a nice guy in a gee whiz, Jimmy Olsen kind of way. It was hard to imagine anyone taking a swing at him.

"What did you do to provoke him?" I asked.

Ross's usually benign expression turned suddenly fierce.

"What did *I* do?" he said. "A guy sends me to the hospital and you think it's because of something *I* did? Did it ever occur to you that maybe the guy is a vicious bully? Did you ever stop to think — "

"Whoa," I said. "Sorry. Bad choice of words. Let me rephrase. How come big bad Jonah Shackleton smashed your jaw?"

Ross looked startled, then grinned sheepishly. "You don't know anything about him, do you?"

"Only what I heard today." I told him what had happened in the cafeteria.

"See?" said Ross. "The guy's a hazard."

"So, what happened between you two?"

"He objected violently to something I wrote about his father."

5

"About the murder, you mean?"

He shook his head. "It's complicated. The bottom line is, when he disagreed with my opinion, he decided to write his letter to the editor with his fist and deliver it in person." He winced, as if the painful memory were still fresh. "He jumped me behind the school and pounded at me like he was trying to kill me. If Eric hadn't come around the corner" — Eric Moore is the school paper's sports editor — "I don't know what would have happened. My face was so swollen that I couldn't open my eyes. I wasn't the first person he attacked, either, so when my parents pressed charges, Shackleton was sent to some youth center for a few months."

"A detention center?" I asked.

"I heard it was more like a group home."

I glanced back over my shoulder at Jonah Shackleton, who was marching up and down, head held high, seemingly oblivious to the people passing him on the sidewalk and the cars passing him on the street. Best to steer clear of him, I told myself.

* * *

"Viens me voir après la classe aujourd'hui, Chloe," Madame Benoit, my French teacher, said to me the next day when I walked into her classroom.

"Oui, Madame."

A couple of years ago, if a teacher had asked me to stay behind after school, I would have assumed I was in trouble. But not anymore, and for sure not in French class in East Hastings. I spent the first fifteen years of my life in Montreal, where even the most determined Anglophones speak passable French. I did way better than that.

When the bell rang, Madame Benoit said to me in French, "I want to ask you a special favor."

"Anything."

"I'm not sure whether you know it, since you are new here, but we have a tutoring program at this school," she said. "We have had great success in enlisting students in the upper grades to help students in lower grades. You are one of my best students. I was wondering whether you might be willing to participate in this program."

I had never tutored anyone before. I wasn't even sure how I would like it, especially if it meant spending a couple of hours a week with some kid in ninth grade. "I don't know . . . " I began.

Madame Benoit smiled at me. "Just think how much you could help someone who is having difficulty with something that comes so easily to you."

What if that student turned out to be as much of a pain as my kid sister Phoebe? Worse, what if the student I was being enlisted to tutor *was* my kid sister? Phoebe was pretty good at school, but she didn't exactly have a facility for language. She could speak the language okay, but it was all street French, and she was sloppy with the basics of grammar and spelling. Madame Benoit wasn't planning to stick me with *her*, was she?

"Well . . . " I said slowly. Did I really want to do this? I looked at Madame Benoit's expectant face. It *was* kind of flattering to be asked. "Okay," I said at last. "I'll do it."

Madame Benoit's smile grew brighter. "I knew you would agree."

"On one condition," I added. She waited. "I don't tutor siblings." There was no way she could have gotten the idea that I could be convinced to change my mind on that.

"But of course," Madame Benoit said, full of understanding. "That will be no problem. The student I have in mind has been absent from school for a while. He has fallen far behind in his studies, but I know he wants to catch up."

That's when I started to get a sinking feeling.

"I have already arranged for him to meet me here tomorrow at lunchtime," Madame Benoit said. "You are free then, yes?"

I nodded slowly. Maybe I was wrong. After all, hadn't she said that the tutoring program involved students in the upper grades tutoring students in the lower grades?

"Good," she said. "Jonah will be grateful, I am sure."

"Jonah Shackleton?"

She nodded and continued to smile pleasantly at me. "Have you had an opportunity to meet him yet?"

* * *

I agonized as I cleared the table that night. I continued to agonize as I pre-rinsed the dishes and stacked them in the dishwasher. I had said that I would participate in the tutoring program, but I had said it *before* I had all the information I needed to make an informed decision. If she had asked me straight out, "Will you help Jonah Shackleton?" I would have said no. Okay, so maybe I wouldn't have come right out and refused. Maybe — probably — I would have made up some excuse: *Gosh, I'd love to help, Madame, but I already have too much to do, what with the newspaper and my own studies and helping out at home.*

"Problem?" said a cavernous voice behind me. Levesque was standing in the doorway to the kitchen. Actually, he filled the doorway. He's a big man, not just tall but wide, like a walking telephone booth.

"Nope, no problem," I said automatically. I can't help it. I don't like people prying into my life without an invitation.

"Then would you mind telling me why you're running the tap full force over dishes that you're going to put in the dishwasher?"

I shut off the water immediately. "Sorry," I mumbled.

He nodded, but he didn't go away. Instead, he stood there and studied me. Before he became chief of police in East Hastings, he had been a police detective. He was always studying people, weighing what they said, trying to decide whether or not they were telling the truth. It made me want to flee to my room, but if I did that, his suspicion would be confirmed and the next thing you knew, I would be telling him what I had been thinking about, which was what I was trying to avoid. Just because you live in the same house as other people, that doesn't mean they have to know every single detail about you, right?

"How are things at school?" he asked.

*Cheeks, don't turn red. He doesn't know anything.
He's just fishing.* "Fine," I said. I was concentrating
on getting my kitchen work done so that I could
retreat to my room.

"You have exams coming up soon, if I'm not mistaken."

"Not for a couple of weeks." From the doorway
there was only silence. Then, thank you, powers
that be, the telephone rang and Levesque scooped
up the receiver. I washed while he talked.

"Yes," he said, "yes, I know. I saw the boy this
afternoon." Pause. "So far as I know, the municipal
bylaws do not prohibit picketing on public property," he said. Was he talking about Jonah Shackleton? "He wasn't blocking pedestrian traffic," he said
in a tone of voice that a stranger might have taken
as reasonable, but in which I, a veteran Levesque
watcher, heard impatience. "As I am sure you know,
Dave — "

Dave? Did he mean Dave McDermott, the may-
or? His office was in the municipal building. He
would have had a clear view of Jonah Shackleton.

" . . . freedom of expression is a charter right. So
long as the boy isn't slandering anyone or engaging
in obstructionist or violent behavior, there's nothing I can do." He was silent for a long time after
that, listening. Then finally he said, "I understand,
but unless the town council comes up with some
way to make it illegal for its citizens to peacefully
express their views, I can't make him stop." More

10

silence, then, "Good night, Dave." He replaced the receiver in its cradle more loudly than usual and — I could be wrong — but I think I heard him say something under his breath.

"Problem?" I asked him cheerfully.

I guess he didn't like people prying into his life either. He looked evenly at me, then left the room. My problem, however, remained. What was I going to do about Jonah Shackleton?

Chapter 2

Have you ever seen one of those cartoons where Donald Duck or Daffy Duck, I forget which one, is torn between helping a rival out of a tough situation and taking advantage of the trouble his rival is in? He can't decide which to do. While he's struggling with his decision, a sweet little angel, all pink and white, lands on his right shoulder and urges him to follow his conscience. "Help the other fellow out. Do what's right because it's right. Goodness is its own reward." For a moment, it looks like he's going to do it, too. Selfish old Donald — or Daffy — is actually going to go against character and do the unselfish thing. Then a plump little red devil appears on his left shoulder, marches right up to his ear, and says, "Don't be a chump. You have to look out for Number One. Besides, what has that guy ever done for you? Do you think if the situation were reversed, he would help you?"

Well, call me Daffy. Or Donald. I couldn't decide what to do. Nobody had a single good thing to say about Jonah Shackleton. He had broken Ross's jaw. He had been ruder to me than anyone I had ever known, and for no reason. Well, okay, so maybe I shouldn't have mentioned his mother, but that wasn't exactly my fault — I didn't know about his mother. I didn't even know him. So why should I help Jonah Shackleton? It didn't seem likely that he would ever help me. After all, he hadn't even wanted to let me sit down across from him in a public place and eat my lunch.

But I had made a promise to Madame Benoit, and I had no quarrel with her. She had always been nice to me. She liked me and I liked her. I had agreed to help as a favor to her, not as a favor to Jonah Shackleton. If I suddenly backed out, she would be the one who was disappointed, not him. Still, drag out all the synonyms you can think of for selfish and vindictive, I didn't want to tutor the guy. So where was my little red devil when I needed him? Because at lunchtime that day, I wasn't in the cafeteria. I wasn't in the newspaper office. I wasn't outside getting some air. Instead, I was trudging up the stairs to Madame Benoit's second-floor classroom. As I prepared to enter the room, I even slapped a smile on my face. In for a penny, in for a pound, as my English teacher — my British English teacher, back in Montreal — used to say.

"Ah, here she is now," Madame Benoit said.

Jonah Shackleton, who was sitting at the desk directly in front of Madame Benoit's, looked up at me. I wished I'd had a camera with me — he looked like a guy who had just found out that his blind date for the prom was his own cousin. When you see someone with that expression on his face, what can you do? You know that figure of speech, grinning from ear to ear? That was me. I was enjoying myself. Because all of a sudden it dawned on me — what could be worse than being tutored twice a week by a person you had been appallingly rude to, a person you wished would stay out of your life, a person you were sure you didn't like? It was great. I was taking the high road and getting even with Jonah Shackleton all at the same time. I was a sinner in saint's clothing.

Madame Benoit looked approvingly at us. She probably saw two well-intentioned young people — one eager to learn, the other eager to help. She made brief introductions, then dove into her lesson plan. I peeked at Jonah a couple of times and saw that he was only half-listening to what she was saying. I would have been willing to bet that what was really on his mind was, how do I get out of this?

"So it's agreed then," Madame Benoit said at last. "If you stick to this schedule, Jonah, you will improve. I have yet to meet a person who works hard and tries hard and does not improve."

Jonah nodded. He tucked his copy of the lesson plan into his binder and put the binder into his backpack. Then he thanked Madame Benoit — in halting, badly accented French — excused himself, and left. I waited a few moments, to give him time to get out of my way, then I packed up my things and left, too. Imagine my surprise when I found him waiting for me in the hall, leaning against some lockers. I thought he was going to say something snide or maybe even yell at me again. But what he actually said was, "We didn't set up a time to meet. What about tomorrow after school, in the school library?"

"Yeah, okay," I said. I waited for more, but he

didn't offer any more. "Aren't you going to apologize?" I asked. He had been a jerk the first time I met him. Now here I was, volunteering to help him. The least he could do was say he was sorry about the gravy stains on my favorite pair of jeans.

"For what?" he said.

I reminded him what he had said and done. He shrugged.

"People who know me know to stay out of my way," he said.

"And people who don't know you are supposed to be psychic?"

Jonah Shackleton actually smiled at me. I suppose I could have been more surprised — if he had responded by reciting a sonnet by Shakespeare. He didn't apologize, though. He just turned and loped away.

* * *

If you're going to walk into a lion's den, it's probably smart to know a little something about lions. What makes them skittish? Under what conditions do they attack? When they look at a human, do they see the big cat equivalent of a bag of potato chips?

Right after school I went looking for Ross, which wasn't exactly like scouring a vast beach for one specific grain of sand. It was always a safe bet that if Ross wasn't in a classroom, he'd be in the newspaper office, which is exactly where I found him. I perched beside his computer and said, "Tell me everything you know about Jonah Shackleton."

"Again with Jonah Shackleton?" he said. "Don't

tell me you're one of those girls who goes for bad boys. You like the dangerous type, Chloe? Like to live on the edge?"

"I got tricked into tutoring him," I said. "Since I have to spend time with him, I'd like to know more about him."

"What do you know about the North Mines Landfill project?"

"The what?" Was he changing the subject?

"North Mines used to be an iron ore mine. Now it's just a bunch of abandoned open pits. There's been a proposal kicking around for the past five or six years to use the pits as a dump for garbage."

"To replace the dump out on Johns Road?"

He shook his head. "Not for local use. The idea is that cities down south that are running out of landfill sites would ship their garbage up here and we'd get rid of it for them — for a price. If you ask me, it's a stupid plan. Those mines were blasted into the water table. Dumping a bunch of garbage into them could contaminate the water supply. But a lot of people in town support it because it would mean more jobs."

All of which was mildly interesting, but, "What does this have to do with Jonah Shackleton?"

"The land that they wanted to use for the site, the North Mines land, was bought by Shackleton's grandfather after the mine was played out. When he died, Shackleton's mother inherited the property. She was offered a lot of money for it — and I mean a *lot* — but she refused to sell. Instead, she decided to give it to an environmental group, which

16

would have guaranteed that it would never be used for a dump site. But she *fell* down her basement stairs the same day she was supposed to sign the land over to the group. The next thing anyone knew, Shackleton's father sold the land to the businessmen who were behind the landfill project. From what I hear, he ended up spending most of what he made on lawyer's fees."

"How long ago was this?"

"Five years."

I was relatively new in town. But I wasn't blind. "Correct me if I'm wrong, but garbage isn't being shipped up here from down south."

"You're not wrong," Ross said. "The project died. It seems some city people have a conscience after all." I tried not to take that remark too personally. "They didn't think it was right to make their garbage someone else's problem. But that doesn't change the fact that Harold Shackleton killed his wife to stop her from giving the land away to the environmentalists when she could have sold it for a lot of money."

I thought about Jonah marching up and down in front of the town hall.

"Jonah seems to think his father is innocent."

"Seems to think? He believes it so strongly that it's practically a religion to him. But, give me a break, his father was tried and convicted."

"So was David Milgaard," I said. "And Donald Marshall. And Rubin Hurricane Carter. And — "

"Yeah, but unlike them, Harold Shackleton had the best motive in the world for the crime he was convicted of — there was a lot of money riding on that landfill deal. *And* he'd been heard arguing with his wife about the land. *And* he had no alibi for the time of the murder. *And* there was no sign of forced entry into the house, no indication that an intruder could have done it. Do you want me to go on?"

Even though I knew he didn't like Jonah Shackleton, the amount of acid in his voice surprised me.

"What did you write, anyway?" I asked.

"Huh?"

"You said you wrote something in the school paper about Harold Shackleton and that's why Jonah beat up on you. What did you write?"

"Last year there was a rumor going around that the North Mines Landfill project would be resurrected — which, in the end, it wasn't. I wrote an editorial that said that when Harold Shackleton committed murder, he didn't just kill his wife, he also killed this town's chance to keep its supply of drinking water clean, not to mention what it would do to the farms south of here that depend on wells that tap into the same water table."

All of this didn't make me like Jonah Shackleton any better, but I was sure starting to get an idea what he was so mad about.

* * *

"Is it true?" Phoebe asked.

I ignored the question. "Pass the salad, please."

"Is what true?" my mother asked.

"Chloe's going to tutor the son of a murderer."

My mother's face seemed to be struggling between a look of concern and one of disapproval. Her daughter in the company of the offspring of a murderer? Wasn't that dangerous? And wasn't it also prejudiced and narrow-minded and politically incorrect of her to assume that it would be dangerous?

"What are you talking about, Phoebe?" my mother said. "Chloe, what's going on?"

"Chloe is going to tutor Jonah Shackleton."

My mother's face was blank.

"You know," Phoebe prompted, a little disdainfully. She prided herself on knowing everything that was going on or had ever gone on in East Hastings, even though we hadn't lived here for long. "Jonah Shackleton's father is Harold Shackleton. Harold Shackleton murdered his wife right here in this house," Phoebe explained. She was actually enjoying herself. "And Jonah Shackleton has spent time in juvenile detention."

"It was a group home," I said, remembering what Ross had told me. Detention made it sound too much like jail.

"Still," Phoebe said, "they sent him there because he kept attacking kids. He even broke some kid's jaw."

My mother finally decided on the appropriate emotion for the situation. She chose concern.

"Chloe, I don't know — "

"It's no big deal, Mom," I said. "Madame Benoit asked me to do it." Mom liked Madame Benoit. They were in the same book club. "I'm sure she wouldn't ask me to do anything that wasn't safe.

And I'm going to be tutoring him in the school library, not in some dark alley. And Jonah didn't do anything except maybe lose his temper a couple of times — "

"He broke someone's jaw!" Phoebe exclaimed.

"It was Ross's jaw and Ross explained everything to me," I said, ignoring Phoebe and concentrating instead on my mother, "so I don't think you have anything to worry about."

"I don't know . . . " my mother said.

"I'll be fine," I said. I even believed it, although, to be honest, now that I knew more about Jonah, I was a little nervous. After supper, after I had cleaned up the kitchen, I stood at the top of the stairs that led to the basement and stared down at the gray concrete floor below. I tried to imagine how I would feel if my mother had been found dead at the bottom. I came up with a few adjectives — devastated, grief-stricken, shattered, heartsick — but they were all just words. Some things had to be experienced to be understood, and, mercifully, I had been spared.

* * *

It takes me nearly thirty minutes to walk to school. Phoebe hates that walk. She wishes there was a bus from our house to the front door of the school. There isn't. Not for kids who live right in East Hastings, anyway. There are buses that bring kids from the smaller towns and from the farms in the area, but townies either have to walk or catch a ride from a parent or friend. I don't mind walking. A brisk thirty-minute walk is good exercise. It's peaceful, too, if you end up spending the whole time alone. You can plan your day, review your homework, or just plain zone out, enter some Zen-like state that leaves you feeling refreshed and ready for anything by the time you're crossing the school parking lot.

I've developed a couple of routes to school, variety being the spice of life and all that. One cuts through the fringes of the provincial park — which was spectacular to look at this past fall when the leaves turned to gold and flame and blood. Another route takes me up and over the railroad tracks — Mom would have a heart attack if she knew. She has a horror of freight trains, which she imagines swoop like ghosts around corners and flatten the kids they surprise. A third route takes me up Centre Street — East Hastings' main street — past all the stores and the municipal building, up the hill past the police station, and up another eternity to the schoolyard. Today I chose the third route.

It was early, maybe eight-fifteen, by the time I was close enough to the municipal building to see that someone — Jonah Shackleton — was walking up and down outside it carrying a picket sign. When I got closer, I saw that this sign was different from the one he had been carrying the other day. This one said, HAROLD SHACKLETON — WRONGFULLY CONVICTED on one side and WHY DOESN'T DAVE McDERMOTT FIND THE REAL KILLER? on the other. Someone else — a guy in jeans and a jean jacket, a guy I sort of recognized, who worked at the gas station just south of the arena — was taking pictures. Or, rather, he was trying to take pictures.

"Hey, man, I don't get this camera," he was saying. "Which button do I push again?"

Jonah looked exasperated. "The black button," he said. "You push the black button."

The guy in the jean jacket lowered the camera to peer at it. "There's a million different black buttons on here," he complained. "I don't get these things. Why didn't you just get a video camera? A video camera you just point and shoot."

"You have any idea how much a video camera costs, Lenny?" Jonah said. "Okay, look, you carry the sign. I'll take the picture."

"Oh, no," Lenny said. "I like your dad, man. You know I do. But I got my probation officer to worry about. All I have to do is stick my big toe across the line and, wham, it's trouble time for me."

Judging from the taut expression on Jonah's face and the way his knuckles grew white around the one-by-two that held his sign, as if he were itching to use it to knock some sense into his friend, I'd say that patience was not Jonah's strong point.

"We're not doing anything illegal," he said. "I told you that a hundred times. All we're doing — "

"All *you're* doing, man."

"All I'm doing is exercising my right to free speech." It was then that he noticed me. It wasn't the warmest greeting that had ever been extended to me. "What are *you* staring at?" he said.

"Me?" I said. "Nothing."

"Yeah, well — "

It was about then that a lot of things happened more or less at the same time. First Dave McDermott, the mayor of East Hastings, flew down the front steps of the municipal building, followed by a skinny guy in a suit who looked like some kind of mayoral assistant, and two beefy guys in security guard uniforms. The two security guards charged at Jonah to grab him by the arms. Correction — to *try* to grab him by the arms. Jonah managed to skip back out of their way.

"Get him out of here," Dave McDermott was saying. "Get him out of here, and get that camera."

The two security guards concentrated on Jonah. The skinny guy in the suit started toward Lenny, who, instead of retreating, drew himself up tall and said, "You touch me, man, and you'll be kissing sidewalk."

For a moment, I felt like I was watching some kind of macho ballet. The two big security guards were circling around Jonah, while Jonah spun in the middle, poking and thrusting with his picket sign to keep them at bay. The mayor was flapping his arms and yelling at his assistant to, "Get that camera, you idiot!" The assistant tried to get hold of it a couple times, but ended up with handfuls of air. Lenny laughed as he held the camera up and out of reach. Then Dave McDermott, fed up, I guess, with the security guards' incompetence, grabbed Jonah's picket sign and yanked at it, trying to free it from Jonah's grip. At the same time, McDermott's assistant, maybe inspired by his boss's example, leaped up at the camera in Lenny's hand like a basketball center trying to score the game-winning basket. Lenny arced his arm back, and I grabbed the camera from him.

"It's okay," I reassured him. "I'm friend, not foe." I don't know why I said that. I sure wasn't planning to take sides. It just came out. "And I know how to work this thing," I added. That did the trick. He relinquished control of the camera to me and turned full on McDermott's assistant. I swung around and clicked a series of great — even if I do say so myself — photos of Mayor Dave McDermott trying to wrestle a *WHY DOESN'T DAVE McDERMOTT FIND THE REAL KILLER?* sign away from Jonah. Then a new face lumbered into the frame. Levesque, with two of his men behind him. Suddenly it was a very crowded stretch of sidewalk.

"All right, break it up," Levesque said, one hundred percent pure cop. He nodded at his men, one of whom stepped between Lenny and the mayor's assistant while the other tapped the two security guards and backed them away from the action. Levesque laid one huge hand on Dave McDermott and the other on the picket sign and, as if he were doing nothing more strenuous than slicing through a spider's web, broke contact between McDermott's hand and the sign. Jonah looked surprised. Maybe he had expected the cops to come down heavy on him.

"Now," Levesque said, peering at the mayor, "does someone want to tell me what's going on?"

I guess Dave McDermott had expected Levesque to go after Jonah Shackleton too, because his face was redder than ever now, and when he answered Levesque, he spluttered, as if the words coming out of his mouth weren't the ones he really wanted to say.

"That boy is marching up and down in front of my office here slandering me," he said. "The last time I checked, slander was against the law."

Levesque listened respectfully — you sort of have to, when you're listening to the mayor — then turned to Jonah. He nodded at the picket sign.

"May I?"

Jonah shrugged and handed the sign to Levesque, who read one side carefully and then flipped it over and read the other.

"I see a statement of opinion on one side and a question on the other, Dave," he said. "I don't see slander."

"Look here, Levesque, you know the political situation as well as I do. I can't afford to have this boy insinuating that I was somehow responsible for a miscarriage of justice — "

One of Levesque's bushy black eyebrows crept up his forehead.

"Is that what you're insinuating, son?" he said to Jonah.

"You bet I am," Jonah said.

Levesque looked at him a moment before turning back to McDermott. I'm pretty sure I saw his moustache twitch, which meant that he was smiling somewhere under it. But that didn't make sense.

"Insinuations aside," he said to Dave McDermott, "the question on this sign does not legally constitute slander. Assaulting this boy, on the other hand — "

"Assaulting?" Dave McDermott thundered. "Are you out of your mind?"

"He's on a public sidewalk," Levesque said, "exercising his right to free speech. He hasn't broken any law — "

"He's defaming me!"

Levesque shook his head. He looked disappointed. "You were a police officer, Dave. You should know the law as well as anyone. You're free to consult a lawyer, but you are not free to take matters into your own hands."

The mayor stepped in close to Levesque and said something in a low voice. I didn't catch the words, but from the tone, I'd say it was a threat. I guess His Honor didn't know Levesque very well. If he did, he would have known that threats never get Levesque to back down. After he had spoken, the mayor spun around. His assistant, looking relieved to have a reason to get away from Lenny, scurried after him. The two security guards retreated.

Levesque handed the picket sign back to Jonah. "It's not my job to give you an opinion on the wisdom of what you're doing," he said. "You're well within your rights with this kind of activity, so long as you keep to public places, don't block the sidewalk, and don't get physical with anyone who might not share your opinions. Do you understand me, son?"

Jonah nodded, but his blue eyes were as cold as a winter's day. I guessed he didn't like cops much. I guessed he didn't want to like Levesque and didn't trust him.

"Okay," Levesque said. "You know what you're up against." He glanced at me then, but said nothing. He nodded at his men and they strode back down the street together, Levesque a half pace ahead. Jonah watched them, then turned to Lenny.

"Did you get any of that on film?" he asked.

Lenny shook his head.

"I did," I said. "I got maybe half a dozen shots." I handed him the camera, then swung away up the hill toward school. I'd get nothing but grief if I brought home a late-slip note for Mom and Levesque to sign.

Chapter 3

You'd think that a guy who could get up at the crack of dawn to walk a picket line — okay, so it was a one-man picket line, which means it really wasn't much of a line — you'd figure a guy like that could manage to get to school on time. You'd be wrong. I looked all day and didn't catch so much as a glimpse of Jonah Shackleton. Which meant that when classes ended and it was time for me to meet him in the library for our tutoring session, I didn't hold out much hope. I stood at the bottom of the stairs, contemplating the two flights up to the library, and asked myself, "Why bother?"

Why? Because never let it be said that Chloe Yan doesn't hold up her end of a bargain. I trudged up the stairs, scanned every inch of the library, and what do you know, still no Jonah Shackleton. Madame Benoit would be disappointed. She had sounded so sure he wanted to catch up. I guess he didn't want it badly enough. Oh well, more time for myself.

I headed back down the stairs and was almost at the bottom when someone behind me yelled, "Hey, where do you think you're going?"

The voice was awfully familiar. I turned and saw Jonah at the top of the stairs, holding the hand — hey, wait a minute, Jonah Shackleton holding a hand? — of a small boy. Then I looked closer and decided that it was the small boy who was doing the holding. Clinging, in fact.

"I looked for you," I said.

"Well, here I am. Jay had a little emergency." With his free hand he tousled the boy's hair, a gentle gesture that surprised me. Then he looked at me and when he spoke, his voice was as hard as ever. "Come on. Let's get to work."

We found a vacant table in a corner of the library. Jonah dumped his backpack onto the floor and helped Jay out of his jacket and smaller pack. He settled Jay into the chair across from his own and the two of them sorted through a small stack of chapter books until Jay found one that he wanted to read.

"You have to be quiet, you understand?" Jonah told the little boy. He didn't look more than six or seven years old. "We're going to be here for an hour." He slipped the watch off his wrist and set it down in front of the boy. "When the little hand lands here" — he pointed to precisely sixty minutes from now — "it will be time to go home for supper. You can let me know when it's time, okay?"

Jay nodded solemnly. He glanced at me, then ducked his head to his reading.

"Your brother?" I said.

"Yeah." Jonah pulled his French textbook and his notebook out of his backpack and opened them on the table. "Okay, let's do it."

It was the most serious hour of group study I have ever experienced. No giggling. No trading jokes. Not a moment of levity. Instead, Jonah concentrated on verbs and tenses and made me quiz him over and over until he could repeat the verb list back to me perfectly. If he kept this up, he was going to be making straight As in no time.

Exactly one hour after we had started, Jay tapped his big brother on the hand. Jonah smiled at him. Once again I was struck by how changed his face was by that simple expression. He closed his books and slid them into his backpack.

"I have to go," he said. "Same time, same place on Monday?"

This was Thursday. "Why not Tuesday?" I said. "Tuesday and Thursday, easy to remember."

He shook his head. "I can't make it on Tuesday." He looked at his little brother, who smiled at him. "Make it Monday. Mondays and Wednesdays, okay?"

I nodded.

Jonah and Jay stood up, put on their jackets, and slung their backpacks over their shoulders, one a tiny version of the other.

"About those pictures you took this morning," Jonah said.

"Yeah?"

"I took them to a one-hour developing place. They turned out pretty good. Thanks."

Thanks? Mr. Surly was thanking me?

"You're welcome," I said.

Jonah and his little brother left the library together, and when they reached the entrance, saw Jay reach up and slip his hand into Jonah's Who would have figured break-your-jaw Jonah

Shackleton could be a sweet-as-pie big brother? It was like Levesque always said, people aren't just one thing, and most people are different things to different people.

* * *

Levesque came home late, after Mom had left for her book club, after Phoebe had gone back to school for a play rehearsal, and after I had assumed he wouldn't be home until really, really late and had spread my geography project out all over the dining room table.

"Sorry," I said when he came in. I started to gather up everything again. "I'll make you some space."

"It's okay," Levesque said. "I'll work around you."

He disappeared into the kitchen and I heard the fridge door open and then, a few moments later, close again. When he returned he was carrying a tall glass of milk in one hand and a cooked chicken leg on a plate in the other. He sat down, careful not to disturb my project, which was turning into a gargantuan topographical map of northern Ontario.

"Looks complicated," he said.

"Mostly it's just time-consuming." According to Mr. Defoe, my geography teacher, cartography is ninety percent art and ninety percent science — which, you're right, you math geniuses out there, adds up to one hundred and eighty percent. Mr. Defoe is quite the comedian. "So, did Mayor McDermott calm down?"

"From what I've been told, Dave McDermott won't calm down until after the next federal election."

"Don't you mean the next municipal election?"

"No, I mean federal," Levesque said. "It looks like there's going to be an election called pretty soon, and from what I hear, Dave McDermott is pretty well guaranteed to get the Liberal Party nomination. Unless the polls change drastically in the next couple of months, he's also pretty well guaranteed to win."

Hmmm. Winning would mean McDermott would spend most of his time far from East Hastings, in Ottawa. "That would mean a new boss for you, wouldn't it?" I said. "So I guess you wouldn't mind if he won." Dave McDermott had a habit of calling Levesque at home about all kinds of minor problems. I had taken a message from him once when he wanted Levesque to tow a car with Manitoba plates out of the mayor's parking space behind the municipal building. On a Sunday. The day of the big fishing competition that drew visitors and tourists from all over. Welcome to friendly East Hastings!

Levesque, as usual, revealed nothing of his feelings. He never gossiped about people, never offered personal opinions about them.

"What's he got against Jonah Shackleton?" I asked.

"Nothing that I'm aware of."

Stupid me. My question had lacked precision. I tried again. "Why is Dave McDermott trying so hard to stop Jonah from picketing? If Jonah thinks his dad is innocent, he has a right to say so, doesn't he?"

"Yes, he does," Levesque said.

"Then how come McDermott wants you to stop him?"

"Dave McDermott was a police officer before he became mayor. In fact, he was the investigating officer in the Mary Shackleton murder. I guess he takes it personally when someone says that he got the wrong man."

"Maybe he did get the wrong man."

Levesque shrugged. "It happens," he said. "But it doesn't happen often. Contrary to what some people would have you believe, the prisons of this country are not filled with innocent men and women. Most people are doing the time because they did the crime."

I trotted out the names of people who had, in fact, been jailed wrongly.

"I said it doesn't happen often," Levesque said. "I didn't say it doesn't ever happen." He finished his milk. The chicken bone lay, picked clean, on his plate. He stood up.

"Do you know much about the Shackleton case?" I asked.

"Only what I've read in the files," he said as he disappeared into the kitchen.

Hmmm, again. I left my map and followed him. I found him bending over to put his glass and plate into the dishwasher.

"Harold Shackleton killed his wife five years ago," I said. "You've only been here for a few months. How come you were reading that particular file?"

Levesque's moustache is so long and bushy that it sometimes takes a few moments before you realize he's smiling.

"You wanted to see what Dave McDermott is sweating about, didn't you?" I said.

He neither confirmed nor denied this. I hadn't really expected him to.

"You went into the files because you wanted to find out whether McDermott had made some gigantic mistake that might cost him his political career, right?"

No comment.

"So, did he? Did he mess up Harold Shackleton's case?"

"I didn't see any evidence of police incompetence, if that's what you're asking," Levesque said. "If I had been handed the same case, I'd have to say that based on what I read, I would have arrested Harold Shackleton too."

I don't know why I was disappointed to hear him say that, but I was.

* * *

A week later, Ross Jenkins said, "Looks like today is going to be the day."

"What day?" I asked.

"The day the town council shuts down Jonah Shackleton." He seemed pleased at the prospect.

"What do you mean?"

"The council is going to pass a bylaw that will make it illegal for anyone to hold a protest or to picket inside town limits without a permit."

"Can they do that?"

34

"With fifty percent plus one, they can do anything," Ross said.

That wasn't what I meant.

"A bylaw like that has to be unconstitutional," I said. "People have a right to express their opinions. You can't just pass a law to stop them." Could you?

"That's where the permit comes in." When he read the blank look on my face, Ross shook his head impatiently. "Don't you read the newspapers, Chloe?"

The newspapers from Toronto? Sure, I flipped through one of those every day, just as soon as I could pry it loose from Mom and Levesque. The local paper? Well, no, generally speaking I didn't read it. Nothing worth reading about ever happened up here, unless you cared about church bazaars, Cub Scout car washes, penny-ante break-ins, and who had just turned ninety-plus years old at the local seniors' residence — none of which interested me.

"Under the bylaw they're going to pass, you can get a permit if you're part of a legitimate organization, like, say, a labor union or a church group — "

"Right, sure," I said. "Those church groups are always out there stirring up trouble."

"Or a legally incorporated nonprofit organization or a legitimate student or youth group — "

"As opposed to an illegitimate one?"

"Legitimate as in officially sanctioned by a school, or an incorporated nonprofit, or a church or church group — "

He sounded like a law book.

"I'm surprised at you, Ross," I said. Surprised and, to tell the truth, a little disgusted.

He drew himself up straight and tall, like a cat arching its back to make itself seem bigger than it really was. "I'm just telling you what the council is proposing."

"You're telling me as if you agree with it. You don't sound even remotely upset, let alone outraged, which, if you ask me, is what you should be. You think this bylaw is perfectly all right, don't you?"

"Why shouldn't I? It's not going to stop anyone with a legitimate cause from expressing their views."

"It will stop Jonah Shackleton from publicly demanding justice for his father."

"Things have to happen in an orderly fashion, Chloe. You can't have people running around saying whatever crazy thing comes into their minds. You can't have chaos."

"Things have to happen in an orderly fashion?" I couldn't believe those words were coming out of Ross Jenkins' mouth. It sounded like something we had studied in history last year. "You mean, like the trains running on time? What next? Bring back Mussolini and his black shirts?"

"Chloe, I think you're overreacting — "

"Democracy isn't orderly, Ross. What if town councils all over North America had stopped people from protesting the Vietnam War? What if Martin Luther King had to get a permit to hold his freedom marches in the South? What if, when women were fighting for the right to vote — "

"We're talking about Jonah Shackleton, not Martin Luther King and Susan B. Anthony."

"If they stop Jonah from speaking out because they don't agree with him, what makes you so sure they won't stop you if you have something to say that they don't like? A principle is a principle, Ross. I can't remember who said it, but it goes like this, '*I may not agree with what you're saying, but I'll defend to the end your right to say it.*' That's what democracy is all about. And I'm stunned that you would turn your back on your principles just because the rights we're talking about are those of a guy who broke your jaw."

"It was wired shut for weeks!"

"I thought you were a better person than that, Ross."

If the newspaper office door hadn't been one of those doors that sighs shut, I would have slammed it.

* * *

I had never been to a city or town council meeting, but I had seen clips from more than a few of them on the TV news back home in Montreal. Most of the time when a city council meeting made the news, it was because the council was considering passing or had just passed some controversial or unpopular bylaw, or was making or had just made some controversial or unpopular decision. Which meant that on the news you usually saw a bunch of angry people at the meeting, shouting at the city councilors and the mayor. I guess that's part of the reason I expected there would be a lot of angry people at this town council meeting. Any way you looked at it, the bylaw that was being considered was wrong. Surely there had to be dozens of people in town who would turn up to say so.

Boy, was I ever disappointed!

Although there was seating for spectators — the public — in the council chambers, only four members of the public were actually present. Well, five, if you counted the old man slumped in a chair in the back of the room, snoring gently. And, technically, I don't know whether you could count one of the remaining four as a member of the public, because he was editor of the local newspaper and, judging from the open notebook in his hand, he was there to cover the meeting. That left three of us: Ross Jenkins, Jonah Shackleton and me. Each of us was surprised to see the other two. I slid into the chair next to Ross's.

"Are you here to cover the meeting, or to speak in favor of the motion?" I whispered in his ear.

He gave me a sour look. "Neither," he said. "I'm here for the same reason you are."

"Oh?" I sounded skeptical. I probably also sounded snotty.

"Okay, so you were right and I was wrong," he said. "I did throw my principles out the window. But I climbed out and retrieved them, okay? I'm here to speak against the bylaw — if they'll let me."

"I'm glad," I said. And I was.

I looked across the room to where Jonah was sitting, alone and staring grimly at the councilors.

I thought about waving him over, but he didn't look in my direction even once, and besides, just because Ross was here defending a principle he believed in, that didn't mean he was ready to be best buddies with Jonah.

The last person to arrive for the council meeting was Dave McDermott. He strode into the room wearing a navy blue blazer and gray pants and carrying a black attaché case. The blazer looked almost military with its polished brass buttons. He took his seat, opened his attaché case, and pulled out a stack of paper and file folders. Then he called the meeting to order.

Before getting to what I considered the main event, the council first debated the desirability of a Tuesday and Friday garbage pickup schedule instead of the current Monday and Thursday pickup. This took the better part of half an hour. Then there was a long discussion about whether East Hastings should start fining people who didn't clean up after their dogs. You have to understand that East Hastings isn't very big. A lot of people take their dogs for long runs on the outskirts of town, and when they do, a lot of them don't bother to scoop up after them. Councilor Ed Jarvis had a property that backed onto the town boundary line, and the back of his yard resembled, in his words, a canine toilet. He was fed up. People paid no attention to the poop-and-scoop signs posted around town. It was, in Ed Jarvis's opinion, time to take the next step. There was nothing like a hit in the pocketbook to show people you meant business.

Through all of this, Dave McDermott remained silent. He looked to me to be more interested in the newspaper he had pulled out of his attaché case along with all the files and documents. He didn't even look up when the garbage vote was taken. Partway through the poop-and-scoop debate, he pulled a handkerchief out of his jacket pocket and spat on it. Then he started polishing the buttons on his blazer.

"Yuck," I said.

Ross glanced at me, a worried expression on his face.

"Not you," I said. "McDermott. He's polishing his buttons with spit."

"Oh," Ross said. If I had to name the emotion in his voice, I'd say it was boredom. "They don't call him 'Spit-and-Polish McDermott' for nothing." This was news to me.

"Spit-and-Polish McDermott?" I said.

"I heard when he was a cop, he kept his uniform buttons so well polished that they almost blinded people on sunny days," Ross said. "My mother says he wears that same jacket to every council meeting. It looks just like a cop uniform, doesn't it?" I nodded. It sure did. "My mom says he doesn't want anyone to forget that he was a cop. And not just any cop. He was the cop who put Mary Shackleton's murderer in prison."

I looked back up at the council table. McDermott was still polishing those brass buttons. He didn't look very cop-like to me. Mostly he looked nauseatingly fastidious.

Finally the proposed new bylaw was raised. It was read and then, to my surprise, a vote was called for without any debate.

"Hey, wait a minute," I said.

Every pair of eyes on the council turned on me. Feeling foolish — Martin Luther King would have been more eloquent than "Hey, wait a minute" — I stood up to give them a better look at me. Then I said, "I don't think you should pass that bylaw."

"Oh?" said a woman I recognized as Camilla Middleton. She was married to the publisher of the local newspaper. "And why is that?"

"Excuse me," said a bald-headed man sitting next to her, "but I don't believe spectators have the right to speak to matters on the agenda unless they are invited to."

"But I have invited the young lady to speak," Mrs. Middleton said. While she spoke, Dave McDermott leaned over and whispered into the ear of the man sitting next to him.

"You don't have the authority to invite her to speak," said the man Dave McDermott had just whispered to. "In order for a member of council to solicit the views of a spectator, first a majority of members of council must vote to allow it."

"Well then, let's vote on it," Mrs. Middleton said.

The next ten minutes were taken up by a debate over whether to allow spectators to speak to this item on the agenda. Finally a vote was taken. Mrs. Middleton lost. Once again a vote was called on the proposed new bylaw. They were going to pass it without hearing even a peep of protest.

"That bylaw is undemocratic," I said loudly. "And refusing to hear what I have to say is also undemocratic."

"You have a lot to learn about democracy, young lady," Dave McDermott said. "We are the duly elected council of this town. We speak and act for the people. Any attempt to impede the work of this council is undemocratic — "

Ross stood up beside me. "People have the right to express their opinions," he said. "If you pass this bylaw, you take that right away. And that's wrong. You can't stifle freedom of speech."

Now the man sitting next to Dave McDermott was on his feet.

"How old are you?" he demanded. "Are you even old enough to vote?"

"I've lived in East Hastings all my life," Ross said. "I have the right to express my views — "

"Do you pay taxes?" the man demanded. "This council represents the taxpayers of this town."

"My parents pay taxes — "

"Get the security guards in here," the man said. "The business of this council will not be disrupted by a couple of kids."

Cue the security guards, the same two who had tried to drag Jonah away last week. Only this time they were coming at me and Ross, and this time Jonah Shackleton was coming to *our* rescue. This didn't stop us from being thrown out of the council chamber, though.

"It's better to have fought and lost than never to have fought at all, I guess," Ross said.

"I suppose," I said. "But this doesn't have to be over just because they're going to pass that bylaw. Laws can always be repealed." I gave Jonah what I intended to be a hopeful look.

"They can pass a million laws if they want to," he said. "But they're not going to shut me up."

"That's the spirit," I said. "Nobody's going to stifle freedom of speech in East Hastings."

Jonah shook his head. "You don't get it," he said. He sounded angry. "This isn't about freedom of speech. This is about justice for my father. And it isn't just my opinion that he's innocent. He *is* innocent. This is about getting him out of prison. They can do whatever they want to try to stop me, but I intend to get my dad out of there one way or another." He turned and walked away.

"You're welcome," Ross called after him. There was a look of disgust on his face when he turned back to me. "You defend a guy's rights and what do you get? A lecture from the guy."

"He believes in his father."

"Yeah, well, no one else does."

I couldn't help thinking, how many people does it take to make a difference?

Chapter 4

Whoever invented public libraries was a genius. I love that you can walk into a public library and go to any of the shelves and pick out books on any subject you can think of and you can take them home and spend the next week or two immersing yourself in them. I love that you can borrow not just books, but magazines and CDs and videos. I love that after school or on a Saturday you can curl up in a library armchair and read newspapers from a half-dozen cities. I love that, if you want to, you can learn about local history by reading back issues of the local newspaper on microfilm. I love that you can book time on one of the library computers and get free Internet access. I think I'd feel cut off and claustrophobic in a small town like East Hastings if the library were to shut down.

The day after the town council meeting, I went to the East Hastings municipal library after school and signed myself up for one of its two microfilm readers. Then I went to the little drawers of microfilm along the back wall of the library, dug out two rolls of the *East Hastings Beacon* from five years ago, fed the first one into the reader and started to read.

I found out that the Harold Shackleton case had been a big deal in East Hastings. In fact, it had been a big deal in the whole region surrounding East Hastings. That's because it was the first homicide in the area since the 1950s. In 1952 an old-time prospector who came into town a couple of times a year for supplies got into an argument with one of the local storekeepers and buried a pickaxe in the guy's skull. In its time, that had been a big deal too.

I read every article I could find on the Harold Shackleton case — and there were lots of them. During the trial, *Beacon* coverage ran for entire pages and included every detail. As near as I could figure out from reading all that ink, what had happened was this:

On June 2, a Thursday night just a little over five years ago, on the eve of Mary Shackleton's death, Harold and Mary Shackleton had argued. They were overheard by a woman who happened to be in the neighborhood — my neighborhood. The woman had been going door-to-door to collect donations for the local humane society. She testified at the trial that from as far away as the street, Harold Shackleton's voice inside the house — my house — sounded like thunder. He yelled at his wife, "You'd better sell that land, if you know what's good for you!" The woman said she went to the door rather than steer clear of the Shackleton house because Harold Shackleton sounded so fierce and because she knew Mary Shackleton and wanted to make sure that she was all right. The woman said that when Harold Shackleton came to the door, he frightened her — he was a big man and seemed angry at her interruption. She said he did not make a donation.

Another woman, a neighbor of the Shackletons, testified that Harold and Mary had been arguing a lot in the weeks before Mary died. She said that on one occasion Mary Shackleton had told her that the arguments were always about the same thing. Harold and Mary quarreled regularly about the money Mary could make if she sold the land her father had left her, land that had been dug deep with open-pit mines. A consortium of businessmen wanted to buy the land and convert it into a dump site for Toronto garbage. The idea was that the garbage would be hauled up to East Hastings by train for disposal. The scheme would have created some badly needed jobs in East Hastings.

The Shackletons weren't poor, the *Beacon* noted, but they weren't rich, either. Harold Shackleton worked at a small auto parts factory an hour's drive from East Hastings. Mary ran the cash register at a local grocery store part-time while Jonah, ten going on eleven, was in school. Harold's sister, who worked in the evenings, looked after Jay, who was two years old. The money from the sale of the land would have come in handy.

Harold Shackleton usually left for work a little before six in the morning, and punched in at his workplace precisely at seven. But on the morning of June 3 — the morning after the humane society canvasser overheard the argument — Harold Shackleton did not follow his usual pattern. According to a statement made to the police by ten-year-old Jonah, Harold was still home when Jonah kissed his mother and left for school at eight o'clock.

I tried to imagine a much younger, much smaller, motherless Jonah telling police what he knew about the morning his mother had died. I tried to imagine how he must have felt doing it.

Harold's sister, Linda, said that Mary called her a little after eight on that morning to say she wasn't going to work that day because she had barely slept the night before. Linda said that her sister-in-law spoke into the phone in a whisper. Mary told her that she and Harold had fought bitterly the night before and that Harold hadn't gone to work yet because, as Mary put it, "I decided we had to settle this land thing once and for all." The paper quoted Linda Shackleton as testifying that Mary had said, "I'm going to tell those businessmen and I just now finished telling Harold, that I've made up my mind. I'm going to sign that land over to Earth Watch this afternoon so that no one will ever be able to dump even a scrap of garbage into those old mines." She had told Linda that Harold was angry with her, but that he "hadn't gone ballistic." She said that while she was speaking to Linda, Harold was upstairs getting ready for work. He had told Mary before he went upstairs, "For heaven's sake, don't go blabbing about our personal business to my sister." Linda said Harold didn't like it when Mary talked to anyone, even a family member, about the state of her marriage and what she and Harold argued about. She said she understood from what Mary said that Harold didn't know Mary had called her.

A couple of hours later, Linda telephoned Mary to see if she wanted to get together for lunch. She got no answer. This worried her. It wasn't like her sister-in-law not to answer the phone when she was home, Linda testified. "I had a strong feeling something was wrong," she told the court. She got into her car and drove the short distance to her brother's house, arriving there at five minutes after eleven. She remembered the time, she said, because the news was just finishing on the car radio when she shut off the engine. Harold's truck was not in the driveway.

She rang the doorbell, but no one answered. The door was locked — unlike a lot of long-time residents in East Hastings, Mary Shackleton always made sure to keep her door locked, something she had learned from her mother, who was once surprised in her kitchen by a would-be burglar. Linda had a key, though, and let herself in — they each had keys to the other's house, she said. She called Mary. In response to her call, she was greeted with what she described as the saddest sound she had ever heard, a pitiful sobbing. She followed that sound to the basement, where she found Mary lying dead in a pool of blood, and little Jay, a toddler, tugging at her arm. Linda said that it looked like he was trying to wake his mother. Linda said she assumed that Mary had tripped and fallen down the stairs and had been killed when she landed headfirst on the concrete floor.

The pathologist who conducted the autopsy came to a different conclusion. He found an injury on the back of Mary Shackleton's head that he declared was not consistent with an accidental fall. Mary

Shackleton had been struck on the head, the pathologist said. That blow had preceded the fall that killed her. Mary Shackleton was the victim of foul play. He also told the police that Mary Shackleton had been dead for a couple of hours.

The local police, in the person of Dave McDermott, began to investigate. Ten days later, Harold Shackleton was placed under arrest for the murder of his wife. In addition to Linda Shackleton, several of Mary's friends testified that Harold and Mary's marriage had become strained over the issue of the old mining land that Mary owned. The Shackletons had argued publicly on several occasions, and those who heard and saw them testified that Harold was angry with his wife over her refusal to sell what he called "useless land." Their differences became even more bitter when Mary started talking about giving the land to an environmental group.

A friend and co-worker of Mary Shackleton's testified that Mary was furious that her husband cared more about himself and his creature comforts than he did about the town and the threat that the proposed landfill would pose to its water supply. Mary had even asked this friend if she knew of any good divorce lawyers. In other words, Harold seemed to have a motive for murder.

There did not appear to be any other likely suspects. No one knew of anyone else who had quarreled with Mary Shackleton. There was no sign of forced entry at the Shackleton house, so robbery was ruled out as a motive. No one in the neighborhood had seen any vehicle other than Harold Shackleton's pickup truck enter or leave the Shackleton property that morning. Reports of exactly when his truck had driven down the street varied by as much as twenty-five minutes. One neighbor thought she had seen the truck at eight twenty. Another put it at closer to eight thirty. Still another swore it was eight forty-five. But no matter how you looked at it — and what proved to be the most critical aspect of the case — Harold Shackleton had no solid alibi.

When first questioned by the police, Harold had said that he wasn't positive, but that he thought he had left for work at a quarter past eight. It never took him more than an hour to get to work, but on that morning he had not punched in at the factory until 10:16 a.m. — an hour later than he should have, given his driving time, and ninety minutes after the latest reported sighting of his truck at his house. This meant there were anywhere from thirty to sixty minutes unaccounted for. Harold explained the discrepancy by telling the police that he had had a flat tire and that it had taken him that long to change it. The police found no evidence of a tire having been removed from the truck, no evidence of a puncture or a flat in any of the tires, and no evidence that a spare tire had ever been installed. When confronted with these facts, Harold changed his story. He said it had taken him longer than usual to get to work because he had argued with his wife that morning. He said he had been so upset by the argument and so afraid that he had destroyed his marriage by insisting that

Mary sell the land that he had pulled over on the side of the road and, as he put it, "cried like a baby."

"I had been thinking only about the money," he said in a second statement to the police, made when they finally arrested him. "I wasn't thinking about my wife, and I was ashamed of that. I promised myself that I would apologize to her the moment I got home. I promised myself that I would ask her to forgive me and that I would always remember that she was more important to me than money." He said that he hadn't told the police the truth the first time because he was embarrassed to admit that he had been crying. He came from a family, he said, where men didn't cry. He insisted that his second statement was the truth.

The crown attorney painted a different picture. He said that Harold Shackleton was a man consumed by greed who cared only about the enormous amount of money he could get for his wife's land. He cared so much that on the morning of June 3, after his son Jonah had gone to school, he argued with her and became so enraged that he struck her on the head. That was the blow that had led to the fatal fall. Much was made of the fact that this had all been done in front of his own small son, Jay, a toddler. Harold Shackleton was a vicious murderer, the crown attorney said, but he was not a clever one. He hadn't planned his crime carefully, and he had been clumsy in covering up his actions. His story about why he was late for work that morning was as sloppy as the crime he had committed. But there was no doubt he had killed his wife.

The jury believed the crown attorney and found Harold Shackleton guilty of murder. He was sent to prison for life, with no chance of parole for twenty-five years.

Dave McDermott ran for councilor in the next municipal election and won. In the election after that, he ran for mayor and won. His political career was still moving forward. With any luck he'd soon be in Ottawa. No wonder he didn't want some kid like Jonah claiming that the police had made a mistake when they arrested Harold Shackleton for murder.

After reading all the newspaper accounts, it seemed pretty obvious to me why Harold Shackleton had been convicted. I could see why Jonah didn't want to believe it, though. If it had been my dad — assuming I knew my dad — I guess I wouldn't want to believe that he could do something so despicable. But it sure made me feel for Jonah. It almost made me want to forgive him for being such a jerk.

* * *

The next Monday when I met Jonah — and Jay, who seemed to be inseparable from Jonah after school — for tutoring, I felt kind of funny. I wanted to talk to him. I wanted to ask him about his father, but I didn't dare. I had a strong feeling that he wouldn't appreciate me prying into his life.

Instead Jonah and I reviewed the difference between *l'imparfait* and *le passé composé*. Jonah had trouble grasping the difference, because in English, whether you say, "I went to school yesterday" or "I went to school when I was young," the verb form is the same. In French — guess what? — it isn't. He got it in the end, though. Then, when our time was up, he did something he had never done before. He said to Jay, "Wait for me outside, okay? I have to talk to Chloe."

Jay didn't move. He stood so close to Jonah that it looked like the two of them were glued together. I wondered, not for the first time, how Jay managed to get through the days at school without his big brother.

"Please, Jay, just go and stand over there," Jonah said. He pointed to a spot across the hall from the library door. "You'll be able to see me. You'll be able to see that I'm not going anywhere without you. I just have to talk to her for a minute, okay?"

When Jay still didn't move, Jonah turned to me and said, "I'll be right back." He took Jay by the hand, led him out of the library, and stationed him across the hall. When he turned to come back, Jay started to follow. Jonah led him back across the hall again, then knelt down and said something to him. I couldn't hear what it was. This time when Jonah came back into the library, Jay stayed put.

"He's always afraid something is going to happen to me," Jonah said. "With Mom gone, and Dad, too . . . " He shrugged. "Anyway, I just wanted to tell you that I appreciate you helping me out with my French."

"No problem," I said, and I smiled at him. "If you

keep going the way you have been, you'll be at the top of the class by the time June rolls around."

"I doubt it," Jonah said. "Anyway, thanks for everything."

I looked hard at him. "What's going on, Jonah?" I had the feeling there was more to this than I was seeing. Although he was saying thank you, he didn't sound like a guy who was simply expressing his gratitude. He sounded more like a guy who was settling his accounts before leaving town. "What are you up to?"

Surprise flickered in his eyes, then he looked away, and I knew for sure that there was something he wasn't telling me.

He looked back over his shoulder at Jay, whose small face seemed etched with worry. "I have to go."

"You're not going to do something stupid, are you?"

"See you around," he said. He ducked out of the library, gathered Jay's hand into his, and away they went, bobbing down the stairs.

* * *

I stood shivering in the dark across the street and two doors down from Linda Shackleton's house. The sturdy brick house had been Jonah and Jay's home ever since their father was sent to prison. I stood and stared up at it for ten minutes, fifteen minutes, twenty minutes, trying to get up the courage to walk to it, climb the steps and knock on the front door. A couple of times I turned away, intending to head home. But for some reason I couldn't make myself do that, either.

This is crazy, I told myself. I barely knew the guy. I didn't even particularly like him — well, that wasn't quite true anymore. He wasn't living down to my first impression of him. He wasn't turning out to be the crazy thug so many people made him out to be. The Jonah Shackleton I had gotten to know over the past little while was a kind and concerned big brother, a determined student of French, and a stubborn believer in his father's innocence. Other than his initial rudeness to me — and if I had just come back from visiting a father in prison, maybe I would have been feeling antisocial too — I hadn't found a single thing about Jonah Shackleton that I didn't like. That didn't mean I knew him, though. He was still pretty much a mystery — but one that I was now determined to figure out.

So stop being a coward and do it, I told myself. Slap one foot down in front of the other and keep on moving forward until you've crossed the street. March up those stairs. Thrust out that hand. Knock.

The woman who answered the door was thin and tired-looking, and seemed vaguely familiar. She was wearing her work clothes — a mint green dress under a white apron. A waitress uniform, I realized. I glanced at the name tag on her chest. No wonder she seemed familiar. She was a waitress at Stella's Great Home Cooking in beautiful downtown East Hastings. I had probably seen her there after school. Seen her, but not really seen her.

"I'm sorry to disturb you," I said. "Is Jonah here?"

She looked at me closely.

"I'm a friend of his from school," I said.

"Friend?" She said it the way she might have said, "Martian?" Then she said, "He's out in the garage." She stared at me a few moments longer, then, shaking her head, closed the door. I headed around the back of the house.

In the light that filtered out through the kitchen window I could see that the dark-colored Chev' that sat in front of the garage had started to rust around the doors and the tire wells. It looked as tired and beaten down as its owner. It also needed a good washing. The garage door was shut, but light shone through a window in the side door. I heard banging from inside, and approached with caution to peep through the window.

Jonah was standing with his back to the door, hammering a nail through some stiff cardboard into a one-by-two length of wood. I waited until he had finished, then I rapped hard on the open door. He spun around to face me, hammer raised as if he were ready to throw it. The surprise on his face gave way to anger when he saw me. He crossed to the door and threw it open. I stepped inside, where it wasn't exactly warm, but it was a little less cold than outside.

"What are you doing here?" he demanded.

I glanced behind him at the black, blue and red markers on his work table.

"Planning another demonstration?" I asked.

"So what if I am?"

"Do you have a permit?"

He gave me a look of withering contempt.

"You were at the meeting, Jonah," I reminded him. "You know it's against the law to picket outside McDermott's office without a permit."

"Yeah?" he said. "So?"

I sighed. So it was going to be like this, was it? He was going to drag out his day-one belligerence and make this hard for me. Did I say hard? If I knew Jonah, he would make it impossible. I reminded myself why I had come. At least, I tried to remind myself. I wasn't so sure I knew anymore.

"I heard what happened last year when you broke Ross's jaw," I said. "I heard there was big trouble, and that it wasn't the only trouble you got into."

He gave me his best butt-out-of-my-life look. "I already have a social worker," he said.

Well, I could be as hard-nosed as him any day of the week.

"Then maybe you need a little legal advice," I said. "Here's some, free of charge. If you picket the mayor's office again, he'll have you arrested. If you get arrested, with your past, you could get into real trouble."

"Since when is that any of your business?"

A very good question from — at that exact moment — a very big jerk. I probably should have listened to him. The trouble is, I can be a very bad listener.

"What if you get arrested and they decide to send you to that group home again?" I asked. "I bet that would be pretty hard on Jay, after everything he's been through."

He came at me then, still holding the hammer. "Get out of here."

I admit it, I was nervous. Everyone said Jonah had a temper. What if he lost control of it now and hit me with that hammer? Except he didn't. Instead, with his free hand he pushed me back toward the door. Pushed me, but didn't push me all that hard. I ducked around him and went over to the work table. There were papers scattered everywhere. I glanced at one. It was a copy of a press release. I scanned it. Jonah grabbed it from me.

"I said, get out."

"Jonah, if you do this — "

"My father is innocent," he said, "but no one believes him. I have to do something. I have to get their attention. I have to make as much noise as I can until someone starts listening."

"But — "

"You can't talk me out of this. You can't do anything. Just go. Please?" He wasn't yelling at me. He wasn't threatening me. He was pleading with me. What could I do?

I nodded. If that was what he wanted, okay.

Chapter 5

"No," Ross said. I hadn't really expected him to say anything different. "No. Absolutely not."

It was an answer I could live with, because with Ross no didn't always mean no. The trouble was, everyone else I asked said no, too. So when the time came — four o'clock on a chilly Tuesday afternoon — and I headed over to the municipal building, I wasn't expecting much.

I managed to be both disappointed and surprised at the same time. Disappointed because Ross wasn't there. Surprised because not only was the editor of the *East Hastings Beacon* standing on the sidewalk, notepad in hand, but so were a couple of other people, also clutching notebooks and tape recorders — more reporters, obviously — and two, count 'em, two!, TV reporters, complete with cameras. Okay, one was from the TV station up in Morrisville and the other was from one of those new cable operations. They were still TV reporters. It looked as though Jonah's press release had worked. I found myself imagining what he could have accomplished if his e-mail access hadn't been cut off. I pulled my sign out of the green garbage bag I had been hiding it in all day and started across the street. Then I spotted Ross. I called to him.

The expression on Ross's face gave him away

before he could speak. Nobody looks that embarrassed when they're about to strike a blow for democracy. I didn't bother to ask where his picket sign was.

The first words out of his mouth were, "I'm sorry," and — I gave him full marks for it — he sounded sincere. "After high school, I'm going to university. Law school, if everything goes according to plan. I can't afford to get into any trouble with the police, Chloe."

A hundred thoughts and words — none of them nice — popped into my mind. I didn't know Ross all that well. I didn't know anyone in this town well. I hadn't been here long enough. But I had hoped for better from him. I headed across the street alone.

Jonah did a classic double take when he saw me and my sign. The FREE COUNTRY, FREE SPEECH side of my picket went well with his FREE HAROLD SHACKLETON. The flip side, FREEDOM OF ASSEMBLY — WRONGFULLY DENIED, was a nice complement to his HAROLD SHACKLETON — WRONGFULLY CONVICTED.

"What are you doing here?" he said. "Weren't you the person who gave me a lecture about the danger of being arrested?"

"That lecture was about the danger of *you* being arrested," I said. "But me?" I shook my head. "I'm not the one who's been in trouble before." Not with the law, anyway. Well, not with the *official* law.

He didn't smile, but he didn't shoo me away, either. We started to trudge up and down in front of the municipal building. Pretty soon one of the TV reporters fell into step beside Jonah and asked him about the town bylaw and why he was defying it. Jonah had obviously done his homework. Either that or he had an innate understanding that television news was all about the sound bite. He answered questions clearly and succinctly:

"An unjust law cannot go unchallenged."

"If this law stops me today, who will it stop tomorrow?"

"My father is an innocent man. Why are some people in this town so afraid to hear me say that? Why is Dave McDermott afraid to hear me say it?"

The street started to fill up. People on their way home from work stopped and stared. Someone, I didn't see who, yelled, "Harold Shackleton is as guilty as sin." The television reporter who had been walking alongside Jonah zipped into the crowd in search of the heckler. Then the doors of the municipal building opened and two security guards emerged — the same two I had met before. Weren't they ever off shift? Behind them was the town councilor who had stopped me from speaking out at the meeting where the bylaw was passed. Bustling up the rear was Dave McDermott, an open coat revealing the spit-polished brass buttons on his navy blue blazer. The press surged toward him, but he thrust out his hands to push them away and bulldozed through the crowd toward Jonah. When he reached him he said, "The police have been called. If you don't put down that sign in the next five seconds, I'll have you arrested."

Jonah responded by holding his sign higher. I moved in close beside him to make it clear that I was not going to be intimidated, either.

Then the cops showed up. That's the cops as in Levesque and a baby-faced young officer named Steve Denby, who had eaten dinner at our house a couple of times a month for the past few months. When Steve saw me standing beside Jonah, he tugged on Levesque's sleeve. Levesque looked at me as if I were a not-very-interesting stranger. I could see he wasn't going to play favorites. He never did.

He came up close to me and Jonah, so close that he blocked what was left of the sun, which wasn't much. I shivered.

"Suppose you put down those picket signs and come with me to the station house so that we can talk this thing over," he said. His voice was low and even, and he spoke slowly and clearly so that we couldn't possibly miss a word of what he was saying.

"Arrest them," Dave McDermott demanded. "They've broken the law."

Levesque held out a hand for the signs. Jonah had to crane his neck a little to look Levesque in the eye. He didn't budge. Neither did I. How could I? Levesque nodded at Steve Denby, who started automatically to reach for his handcuffs, then hesitated. He looked at Levesque for confirmation. Levesque shook his head. Steve Denby put his cuffs away and instead started to steer Jonah up the street. He was closely followed by the photographers and camera operators. Levesque lay a hand on my shoulder, where it sat, as heavy as stone, all the way down the street.

I had been inside the police station often to get Levesque to sign school permissions I had forgotten to get from Mom, or to hit him up for a few dollars when I had run out of allowance. But I had never been there on official police business.

"Am I under arrest?" I asked.

Levesque didn't answer. He closed the door firmly behind us to keep the press out. Then he directed Jonah into a chair. He was just waving me into another when the office door opened and Dave McDermott exploded into the room, followed by his assistant and the councilor who had stopped us from speaking at the meeting. Dave McDermott marched up to Jonah and bent over him until his nose was almost touching Jonah's.

"You're in trouble now," he said. "You can't go around saying whatever you want about people and trying to smear their good names. There are laws in this town, and they're going to be respected." He spun around to face Levesque. "Tell him, Levesque. Show him what it means to be under arrest."

"I don't think that's a good idea," Levesque said. He said it in a kind of offhand way, and not with the tone that you might expect if you were the mayor and had issued what you probably considered a direct order.

Dave McDermott stiffened. "These kids have broken the law. It's your job to arrest law-breakers, even if one of them is your daughter."

Jonah looked over at me. If I had been forced to name the emotion I saw on his face, I would have said it was betrayal, with maybe a little hatred mixed in. He started to get up out of the chair. Levesque dropped a hand onto his shoulder and eased him back down.

"The law you want me to enforce is not a good one," Levesque said to Dave McDermott.

"The law I want you to enforce was passed by the duly elected representatives of this municipality," His Honor said. "And as I'm sure you know, the Municipal Act allows municipal councils to pass such laws as they see fit to protect the health, safety and welfare of their citizens."

Levesque looked evenly at Dave McDermott. Then he steered McDermott, closely followed by his assistant and the councilor, toward the door that led out of the main office to the back hall. Just then a couple of reporters pushed through the front door. Steve Denby went over to block them from coming in, and ended up going outside with them — which left me with an opportunity. I crept over to the door that led to the back hall and pressed my ear against it. I could make out the deep rumble of Levesque's voice.

"And as I'm sure you know," Levesque was saying, "anyone can apply to the Supreme Court of this province for a review of any bylaw. The one council just passed almost certainly contravenes the Charter of Rights and Freedoms, specifically Article 2, the fundamental freedom of peaceful assembly."

He sounded calm in contrast to Dave McDermott's usual bluster.

"There are reporters and cameras from two television stations out there, Dave," Levesque said. "They might look at the bylaw as less a matter of protecting the health, safety and welfare of East Hastings residents and more a matter of protecting the health, safety and welfare of a certain ex-police officer's political aspirations."

There were a few moments of silence. I pictured Dave McDermott conferring with his assistant.

"Then, with all due respect," Levesque said, but I didn't hear a lot of respect in his voice, "the bylaw that council passed was ill-conceived. I am, frankly, astonished that it was taken seriously enough to be voted on, let alone carried. This town's legal counsel — and I'm assuming you had the bylaw vetted by counsel before you voted on it — must have been asleep at the wheel. The bylaw is unlikely to stand. It may take a while before someone comes forward with a legal challenge to it. In the meantime, though, both the bylaw and the council that passed it are probably going to get a whole lot more press — none of it favorable. And if you get the nomination and run in the next election, whoever runs against you is guaranteed to make a big stink about all of this. I'm sure even you can picture the headlines, Dave."

More silence. Then Dave McDermott said, "Maybe it would be better for all concerned if you let these youngsters go with a warning." The doorknob turned. I skidded over to the coffee machine that sat on top of one of the filing cabinets, and fumbled for a cup.

Dave McDermott didn't even look at me as he went by, but Levesque did. It was a very sharp look. Dave McDermott, trailed by his assistant and the councilor, reached the front door at the same time as Steve Denby. They all did a little waltz until everyone who wanted to get out was outside and Steve Denby was back inside with the door closed again. Then I said to Levesque, "What just happened?"

Levesque looked evenly at me. "It turns out the mayor is more interested in constitutional rights than I gave him credit for," he said.

Steve Denby laughed out loud.

In other words, now that the press had taken an interest, sticking to this law to silence Jonah Shackleton's claims about his father's innocence would only hurt Dave McDermott. Good.

"Does this mean we can go?" I asked.

Levesque nodded. "I suppose it does."

I waited for one of Levesque's famous lectures. He didn't deliver one. Instead he sat down at his desk and pulled a file from his in-basket. I didn't understand his restraint, but that didn't stop me from being grateful. I looked at Jonah.

"What do you say we get out of here?"

Jonah was on his feet before I had finished speaking. He strode over to the door ahead of me and plowed through the press outside. He didn't stop to try to charm them or sell them on his point of view. I had to run to catch up with him.

"Hey, what's wrong?"

He turned on me, looking ferocious.

"The top cop around here turns out to be your father? Funny you didn't mention that."

"He's not my father. He's my stepfather."

"Whatever."

"It's not a big deal," I said.

"It is to me. I don't like being made a fool of."

Okay, now he was making me mad. "And just how do you figure I made a fool of you?"

"I thought you cared about what I was doing. I thought — " He broke off. A dozen emotions seemed to be battling for control of his face. Betrayal won. "I thought you were on my side."

"I am." At least, I was enough on his side to believe in his right to say what he wanted.

"Your father is a cop."

"My stepfather," I repeated. "And so what? He didn't have anything to do with what happened to your dad. The worst thing you could accuse him of is stopping you from being arrested and getting into even more trouble."

He stared at me. It looked to me as if he were groping for something nasty to say. In the end, though, he simply wheeled around and stalked away. I should have let him go. Ingrate. The more I helped him, the angrier he seemed to get with me. Who needs that kind of grief? Let the guy stew in his own juices, as my mother liked to say — a little something handed down to her by her mother. Let him stew — that would have been the smart thing to do.

"Besides, Einstein," I called after him, "it's not like this lame plan of yours is going to get you anywhere."

He slowed the pace of his retreat. He turned. He glared at me — it was getting to be his favorite expression — hands clenched at his sides.

"I'm doing everything I can to get attention for my father's case," he said. "I sent e-mail to everyone I could think of — lawyers, newspapers, television stations, radio stations, that group that is supposed to be helping people who were wrongfully accused — you name it. And you know what happened?" I did. "I got my computer privileges taken away at school. My aunt is a waitress. She doesn't have a lot of money. She can't afford to buy me a computer. So you know what I did? I got my mom's old typewriter out of Aunt Linda's attic and started sending letters. Dozens of letters. I've contacted everyone I can think of — "

"And what exactly are you offering them?" I asked. "My dad didn't do it? My dad is innocent? Do you really think if you march up and down the street long enough saying he didn't do it, people will start to believe you? They won't. It's not going to help, either, if you keep making enemies all over town with all your hostility and in-your-face protests. And for sure you won't get anywhere if you spend all your time and energy dumping all over the small handful of people who are willing to help you."

I had said about a hundred angry words. His response was just one: "How?"

"Huh?"

"How do you suggest I go about getting my father out of prison?"

Good question. One to which, unfortunately, I hadn't given much thought.

"Well, if your dad is innocent, then what really happened? The medical examiner said it was a blow to the back of her . . . " Boy, did I ever not want to be saying this, to be talking about his mother. ". . . to the back of her head that sent her toppling down those stairs." He seemed surprised that I knew the details. "You have to ask yourself, If your dad didn't do it, then who did?"

He waited for a moment, peering intently at me. Then he said, "Well? Who did?"

"That's what we have to find out, Jonah."

At first his expression didn't change. Then he blinked. "We?"

The word had just popped out. I'm not sure why. Maybe it was seeing how determined he was. Maybe it was the way Jay was always holding his hand, like he was depending on Jonah to make everything okay. Maybe it was because I wanted to see Jonah smile again, I wanted to get to know the person he was when he wasn't angry with the world, and I knew that wasn't going to happen until he figured out the whole story about his parents. Whatever it was, now that I had said it, it sounded right.

"We," I said emphatically.

Chapter 6

After supper my mother grabbed her book, her book notes for her book club meeting, and the car keys.

"Can you give me a lift?" I asked.

She looked surprised. "Where are you going?"

"To the library," I said, and added quickly, since it was a school night, "to study."

She glanced at her watch. "Okay," she said, "but we have to hurry. The meeting is at Jeanne's house."

Jeanne was Madame Benoit. She lived a few miles out of town in a big old brick house.

When I told my mother I was going to the public library to study, it was only half a lie. I did go to the library. Jonah showed up about five minutes after me, but instead of heading upstairs for a study session at one of the big work tables, we went to the small room in the basement that contained four vending machines and three small tables. The room was deserted. We sat across from each other at one of the tables, and I pulled a notebook from my bag.

"Okay," I said. "I guess we should start with the basics. Who had a grudge against your mother?"

At first Jonah said nothing. He just stared at me. Then, "You're serious, right?"

"Serious about someone having a grudge against your mother?"

"Serious about finding out who killed my mother."

"I am." And I was. But what I didn't tell him was that it was quite possible — in fact, it was probable — that what we would find was that Levesque was right and that Jonah's father fell into the same category as almost everyone else in prison. Despite what he had told Jonah and despite what Jonah himself had chosen to believe, it was possible — in fact, it was probable — that Harold Shackleton had actually killed his wife. Maybe Jonah needed to come to grips with that. "So," I said, "who didn't like your mom?"

He reacted as if I had slapped him across the face, and his reaction made me feel as if we had just crossed swords in a duel.

"Everyone liked her," he snapped. "You didn't know her, but my mother was a great person. She only worked part-time, even though we could have used more money, because she wanted to make sure that Jay and I got a good upbringing. She volunteered at the seniors' residence two evenings a week. She was interested in environmental stuff — she was always after us to recycle and to not run the water so much."

It was hard to find the right words to talk about this.

"Someone must have had a reason to hurt her, Jonah," I said as gently as I could.

His nostrils flared. "My mother was the kindest, sweetest person you'd ever want to meet."

"I'm not saying she wasn't." I kept my voice low — a trick I had learned from Levesque. Talk low and people have to work at listening to you. It also tends to make them stop yelling. "But someone killed her. That's what this is all about, right? Someone killed her and — I could be wrong — but it was probably someone who had a grudge against her. Someone besides your father."

"My father didn't have a grudge against my mother."

"They argued a lot over whether or not to sell some land your mother owned, didn't they?" When he looked as if he were going to shake his head, I said, "Four or five people testified at your father's trial that they had heard them arguing. One of your mother's friends said your mother was so angry with your father that she even asked about a divorce lawyer."

"She wasn't serious."

I looked into his blue, blue eyes. "Do you know that for a fact or do you just hope she wasn't serious?"

Talk about poking an already enraged Rottweiler. He swept to his feet.

"Are you saying I didn't know my own mother?"

Stay calm, Chloe. Make him listen.

"You were, what, ten years old at the time?"

"Almost eleven."

"How much does any ten- or eleven-year-old really know about his parents' lives? People heard them fighting. Your own aunt testified at the trial that your mother was very unhappy with your father for trying to pressure her into selling her land to developers. Other people, friends of your father, testified that he was angry with your mother for refusing to sell."

"You're saying my father did it, aren't you?"

"I'm saying people — the twelve people on the jury, in particular — believed that your father had a strong enough reason to kill your mother that they convicted him of murder. I'm saying, if he didn't do it, then someone else must have, and if someone did, whoever it was must have had a reason. And I'm saying that if you have any ideas about who that someone might be, it could really help."

He nodded slowly and just as slowly sat down. I sat quietly, watching him until, finally, he shook his head.

"Everyone liked Mom," he said. His lips were firmly set, as if he were trying to keep control of himself. "Everyone liked her a lot." He closed his eyes tight. Then he said, "Maybe it was a stranger."

"According to the newspaper coverage of the trial, the doors to the house were locked and there was no sign of forced entry. Anyone who went into the house got in because they had a key, or because your mother let them in." I left out the alternative — that the murderer was already in the house. "That's why the police concluded that the killer was someone your mother knew, and, if you ask me, that makes sense."

His temper exploded again and he stood up abruptly, sending his chair scudding backwards.

"And because everyone liked my mom and no one except my father had a reason to kill her, then my father must have done it, is that it?"

"Jonah — "

"Forget it, okay? Just forget the whole thing!"

He stomped out of the room and down the hall to the stairs. This time I didn't try to stop him. I listened as his footsteps grew fainter and fainter. Only then did I gather my things together and leave the building.

On the way home, as I passed the municipal building, I saw Dave McDermott walking a woman toward a car. A good-looking woman. He guided her around to the driver's side and opened the door for her. After she got in, she rolled down her window and stuck her head out. Dave McDermott bent down and kissed her on the cheek. Hmmm, I thought, is the mayor soon going to have a missus?

* * *

"What if," I said to Levesque right after I got home, "you were one hundred percent positive someone didn't commit a certain crime, but you had no proof that could help clear that person? What would you do?"

Levesque lowered his newspaper and barked. At least, that's what it sounded like. While he was looking at me and considering my question, I heard another bark, only this time I was pretty sure it hadn't come from him. It sounded as if it had come from the basement. There it was again. A big, deep *rowf!*

"Is there a dog in the house?" I asked.

Levesque surprised me by responding with a nod. "Your mother brought it home from her book club. She's downstairs now, trying to settle it into a bed."

74

Whoa! "Mom brought a dog home?" In my whole life so far, the only living creatures that had shared any place I called home had been my mother, my sisters and me. And, recently, Levesque. No dogs, no cats, no birds, no hamsters, no goldfish. Strictly people.

"She found it wandering out near the highway. It looks as though it was abandoned."

"Abandoned? And Mom brought it home?"

"She said she felt sorry for it."

"For a dog?" Don't get me wrong. It's not that I thought my mother was hard-hearted. It's just that, well, I had never thought of her as a pushover for any creature that didn't walk on two legs. Two people legs.

Levesque shrugged. "She says she wants to keep it. I guess we're going to have to go along with that."

The dog barked again.

"He's not going to do that all night, is he?" I asked.

"I sincerely hope not. And he is apparently a she. Now, what were you asking me?"

I repeated my question.

"Without any evidence to the contrary, why would you be so sure this person didn't do it?" he said.

"How about, innocent until proven guilty?"

"A fine principle," Levesque said. "Only in this case, unless I'm mistaken, we're talking about someone who *was* found guilty."

"The evidence was circumstantial," I pointed out. "I read the newspapers. There were no eye-witnesses." Well, Jay Shackleton had seen it. He had been found beside his mother. But he was just a toddler at the time and, besides, the papers said, leaving aside the fact that he would have been far too young to ever testify in court, he had been so traumatized that he hadn't been able to tell the police anything. "There was no physical evidence that linked Harold Shackleton to the murder." See what having a cop in the house does? It makes you talk like a character on a TV police show. "They never found the object that was used to hit Mary Shackleton on the back of the head or even figured out what it was. And because they never found it, there was nothing that physically tied Harold Shackleton to the murder weapon."

"They did, however, determine that Harold Shackleton had a motive for murdering his wife," Levesque said. "The house was locked when Mary Shackleton's sister-in-law arrived and there was no sign that any of the locks had been forced or that any of the windows had been tampered with. Other than Linda Shackleton, no one else besides Harold and Mary Shackleton had a key to the house, and without a key, the only way the killer could have entered the house was if Mary Shackleton had let him in. All the locks in the house are deadbolts, which means that for the doors to all be locked when Linda Shackleton showed up, the killer would have had to let himself out and then lock the door after himself, something that he could only do if he had a key. But all the keys to the house were accounted for — Harold Shackleton had his on his keychain, Linda had hers to let herself in, and Mary's was found in her purse."

"Maybe Linda Shackleton killed Mary," I said. Of course I knew even as I was saying it that it was lame.

"At the time of the murder, Linda Shackleton was driving a six-year-old Mustang with a bad muffler. She had already been ticketed twice for it. Someone would have heard her drive up to the house even if they hadn't seen her car. The neighborhood was canvassed. No one heard or saw anything. Besides, after she found out that Mary didn't need her to babysit, Linda went into town to get her hair done." Then, before I could speak, he added, "And, no, she couldn't have gone to the house, pushed her down the stairs, and then calmly called the police. Linda Shackleton arrived at the house at five minutes past eleven. Dave McDermott arrived at twenty past eleven. The coroner was there less than an hour later. She determined — and this was confirmed when the autopsy was done — that Mary Shackleton had been dead for several hours. So Linda couldn't have done it."

It was clear he had done more than read the Harold Shackleton file. He had memorized it.

"Okay," I said. My head was spinning. "Okay. But suppose you still believed Harold Shackleton was innocent. What would you do?"

"Chloe — "

"Imagine it was Mom," I said. "Imagine Mom had been convicted of killing someone and it looked really bad for her. But imagine that for some crazy

77

reason you believed her. What would you do?"

"Find someone else with a motive, I guess," he said. He didn't sound too happy about it.

"Like?"

He shook his head. "You're the one who's second-guessing the courts," he said. "If you want to know more, you'll have to get out a shovel and start digging. There are no shortcuts in criminal investigation."

Thank you, Chief Levesque.

The dog barked again. Loudly. Several times. Maybe a dozen times. Mom obviously wasn't having much luck in the settle-Rover department. A few moments later the door to the basement opened and I found myself almost bowled over by the big golden-colored dog. I got down on my knees and started to scratch her behind the ears. She settled down. When I stopped scratching, her paw came up and tapped me on the hand. I scratched her some more, then stopped. Up came her paw again.

"She's obviously had some training," Levesque said. "I guess that's a good sign."

"She obviously doesn't want to sleep in the basement," Mom said. "That's not so good."

I looked at the dog's dark brown eyes. When I stood up, she watched me. When I started for the stairs, she followed. When I turned around to face her, she stopped. I'd never had a dog before. I wasn't even one hundred percent sure that I liked dogs. But it made me feel sort of special that she wasn't sticking to Mom, who had rescued her. Nor did she seem particularly drawn to Levesque. It was me she wanted to follow.

"I guess she can sleep in my room if she wants to," I said. "You know, until she gets used to being here."

My mother looked at Levesque. Levesque looked at me.

"At least she isn't barking any more," he said.

* * *

I should have been studying for a chemistry test. Instead, I lay on my bed and tried to figure out *how* to figure out who had killed Mary Shackleton. Actually, I lay on half of my bed. The dog — she needed a name — had staked a claim to the other half. Take Harold Shackleton out of the picture. Take him at his word. Take it as given that he hadn't committed murder. Who did that leave?

Not Jonah's Aunt Linda, that was obvious. What about other relatives? Maybe someone else in the family had been pressuring Mary Shackleton to sell the land and give them some of the money. But if that were true, surely it would have come up at the trial. Surely Harold Shackleton's lawyer would have mentioned it.

Okay, maybe it was something completely different. Maybe Mary Shackleton had a boyfriend. After all, she and Harold had been fighting pretty much nonstop. Maybe Mary had gotten sick of Harold. Maybe she had started seeing someone else. Oh yeah, brilliant, Chloe. What does that do? That gives Harold one more reason to want to kill his wife. Back to basics. The main motives for murder are: rage, jealousy, revenge, profit. Which pointed to . . . Harold, Harold, Harold, Harold.

The land seemed to be the key to the case. Harold wanted Mary to sell the land so that he — and she — could get rich. That meant the motive was profit. Then, when Mary told Harold instead that she meant to give the land away to a bunch of tree huggers, rage entered the picture and he killed her, knowing that the land would go to him instead, as beneficiary of her estate. It had to be about the land and money. Rage and profit.

Mary had been offered a lot of money for the land.

Therefore, the land was worth a lot of money.

Hmmm.

The land had been worthless for years and now it was worth enough to kill for. Why was that? Because before, no one had wanted it, and then, suddenly, someone did. Someone wanted to turn the land into a landfill site. Dump sites were in short supply near big cities like Toronto. So, if someone was ready to offer Mary Shackleton a lot of money for that land, that same someone must have thought he — or she, or, I suppose, they — could make even more money from it. You don't offer to pay a lot of money for something unless you're pretty sure you can squeeze even more money out of it.

Hmmm.

So, imagine a person who had his — or her, or their — heart set on buying Mary Shackleton's land so that he — or she, or they — could make a fortune. Maybe he — or she, or they — managed to sell this project to people down south, and they were all excited. So now this person was really convinced that millions of dollars were just waiting to line his pockets. There was one problem, though. Mary refused to sell. So maybe the person who had his heart set on buying the land got angry. Maybe just as angry as Harold Shackleton. So maybe that person had a pretty strong motive for murder — well, assuming there weren't a dozen other properties around that could be bought and used for the same purpose.

And hadn't Ross said something about the new jobs that would be created if the dump project went forward? If there was one thing East Hastings could use, it was more jobs. So maybe there were a few more someones who had it in for Mary Shackleton, people who didn't like the fact that Mary Shackleton was the obstacle to new jobs coming to East Hastings.

I hadn't made much progress, but at least I had unearthed some possibilities. The trouble was, I had no reason to think that someone else, then-police-chief Dave McDermott, for example, hadn't thought of these possibilities too. Thought of them, investigated them, eliminated them. Which gave me one more thing to check into.

I heard a funny snuffling sound next to me. I turned to look at the dog. Her eyes were closed. Her body was rising and falling as she breathed languidly in, then out again. The big golden dog was sound asleep — on my bed.

81

Chapter 7

"What is it with you?" Ross said. He clicked to save the article he had been working on, then turned away from his computer to look at me. "You believe him, don't you? That's what this is all about. Despite all the evidence to the contrary, despite the opinion of twelve people who served on the jury that convicted Harold Shackleton, you believe Jonah Shackleton when he says his father is innocent."

"Maybe I'm just keeping an open mind."

"An open mind about an open-and-shut case?" He shook his head. "Did it ever occur to you that Jonah is in total denial? Back when it happened, everyone made a big deal about his little brother being right there and seeing his mother being murdered — I heard the kid was so traumatized he didn't say a word to anyone for something like two years afterwards. But if you ask me, Jonah got himself messed up over this too. He's never admitted that there's even the slightest possibility his father did it. He's been getting into fights over this since sixth grade. He's nuts."

"If you were accused and convicted of murder and you said over and over that you hadn't done it, who would you want your parents to believe — you or everyone else?"

He opened his mouth to answer, but no words

came out. Ross can be opinionated. He can be infuriatingly arrogant. He can batter you into the ground with his arguments if he's convinced he's right. But he's also fair. Well, pretty fair. If you put a reasonable question to him, he will consider it carefully.

"I guess I'd want them to believe me, but . . . "

"Flip that around and you've got Jonah and his dad."

Ross sighed. "Okay. What is it you want to know?"

"It's about the landfill project. I don't understand why Mary Shackleton's property was such a big deal. There must be hundreds of places up here where the same kind of dump could be located. Her land wasn't the only land that could have been used, was it?"

Ross peered at me as if he were trying to figure out where the answer to this question would lead me.

"I know it looks like there's nothing but empty land up here," he said, "but that isn't exactly true. First, there's East Hastings Provincial Park." This was a large government-protected wilderness park. "You can't put a dump in there. And you can't put a dump in most of the places right around it, either, because it would be disastrous if the park's water system became polluted. On top of which most of the land around here is Canadian Shield. It's just a thin layer of topsoil over yards and yards of solid rock. You can dump garbage on top of it, but dump garbage *in* it?" He shook his head. "First you'd have to dig — forget dig, you'd have to blast — an enormous pit. That costs money. You'd also have to build a road to the site. That's why the abandoned open-pit mines seem perfect. They're great big deep holes in the ground and there's already a road leading to them. Their main attraction is that they're there. It has nothing to do with whether or not they're suitable."

"So it was Mary's land or no land for the dump site?"

Ross nodded.

"How did Jonah's grandfather end up owning the property?"

"Apparently old Claude LaCasse — that's Jonah's grandfather on his mother's side — was a little nuts. They say the company sold the property to him for next to nothing, so that if it turned out that there was any damage to the water table, *he* would be responsible as the owner, and the *company* would be off the hook. When the North Mines Landfill project came along, Claude must have thought he had died and gone to heaven. I heard that the group that wanted to turn the mines into a landfill spent over a million dollars developing the plan for the site and selling it to all those politicians down in Toronto. And they promised Claude a lot of money for the land as soon as they got all the approvals they needed. Unfortunately for them, Claude died. Mary inherited the land, and then refused to go along with the deal."

"Do you have any idea who the people were who wanted to buy the land?"

"A group of businessmen," Ross said. "Why?"

"Do you know who they are?"

He arched an eyebrow. "Maybe this is a good time to remind you that, at the time of Mary Shackleton's murder, I wasn't much older than Jonah. I was eleven years old."

"You sure know a lot about the history, though."

"I took an interest in it when it looked like the project was going to be resurrected."

"So, do you know who these businessmen are?"

Ross shook his head. He let me stew in disappointment for a few moments before he said, "But I know how I can find out, if you want."

I waited. So did he. He wanted me to ask.

"How can you find out, Ross?"

"My mother is the municipal clerk."

"She is?"

"Yeah," Ross said. "And, by the way, thanks for taking an interest in my life."

Ouch. I had known Ross for five months now, but I didn't know as much about his family as he knew about mine. I hadn't asked.

"There must be some records somewhere," he continued. "They probably would have had to apply for some permits. I'll ask her and get back to you, okay?"

I knew how much he disliked Jonah, so for sure he wasn't doing this as a favor to him. Which meant he was doing it for me.

"Thanks, Ross," I said. "I really appreciate it."

He made a sour face, but nodded. Then he went back to his article.

He got back to me a lot sooner than I expected. He was waiting for me outside school the next morning, ears red from the November cold, a sheet of paper clutched in his hand.

"Got 'em," he said, waving the paper.

I took it from him and scanned the list — seven names and addresses, four of them in Toronto and three of them up here in this area.

"Do you know any of these people?" I asked.

"Can we go inside?" His teeth were chattering like castanets. I wondered how long he had been standing out in the cold, and why. He could have waited for me inside the school, where it was nice and warm. But when I asked him about it, all I got for an answer was a shrug. We went down to the newspaper office where we could sit and warm up. I waited until Ross's ears faded to their normal color before I asked my question again.

"I'm way ahead of you," he said. "I had an idea what you'd want to know, so I got my mother to fill me in. And, by the way, I told her it was for an article I'm working on. I didn't mention Shackleton's name." When I looked puzzled, he explained. "The municipal clerk's office is in the municipal building, where the mayor's office is. It's not that big a municipality, so it's not that big an office. People talk. I figured you probably didn't want anyone making any more trouble for your friend Jonah." There was an edge to his voice when he said the word friend, but I let it go. He was trying to be nice and mostly he was succeeding.

"This guy," he said, poking at the list, "Bob Chartoff, owns a garbage hauling business — seven trucks that pick up garbage in fourteen towns in this region. No surprise there — I guess it's natural a garbage guy would want in on a garbage dump business. The second guy, Fred Simla, is a vice president at the car parts plant where Harold Shackleton used to work."

That was interesting. "He must have known Harold," I said.

"I guess. The last guy, Norman Himmel, is an accountant for a car dealership. He lives in Morrisville." He looked over at me. "So, now what?"

Good question.

Ross studied me for a moment and then said, "You're thinking maybe one of them could have killed Mary Shackleton, right?"

"Any of them might have had a motive," I said, "depending on how important the dump site was to them. And depending on where they were the morning Mary Shackleton was killed and whether or not they had access to a key to the Shackleton house." And whether or not they had an invisible cloak to get them into the house without being seen, I thought. I didn't say it, though. I didn't have to because Ross was already giving me a strange look.

"Look, I know you figured out what happened to Peter Flosnick," he said, "but if that's the best you can come up with, then maybe you're losing your touch."

"You're saying it's a stretch?"

"It's a stretch even Shaquille O'Neal couldn't

make. But then — " He broke off suddenly.

"But what?" I asked.

"Nothing."

"Say it."

"Never mind."

"Ross," I said sternly.

"Okay. It's an even bigger stretch to think that Harold Shackleton didn't do it."

"I know," I said. He wasn't saying anything I hadn't considered.

"Then why are you wasting your time on this?"

We were sitting in the main room of the newspaper office with our backs to the door, which was why neither of us saw who was opening the office door. I wish I had turned to look before I answered.

"I guess I feel sorry for Jonah," I said. "He lost his mother and his father, and he's obviously having trouble dealing with that. He's angry at everybody. He thinks the whole world is treating his father unfairly. Maybe if he works out for himself what really happened, even if it's not the answer he's looking for, maybe it will help him. I've been thinking — "

By this time, I had noticed that Ross wasn't listening to me. He had glanced over his shoulder, and he hadn't looked back at me. He nudged me.

"What?" I said, annoyed that he wasn't giving me his undivided attention.

He gestured toward the door. I turned just in time to see it close. I looked back at Ross.

"Jonah," he said. "Jonah was standing right there."

It's possible that I had moved faster at some point in my life, but I couldn't think when. I jumped up and raced out of the newspaper office. The basement corridor was empty, but I heard footsteps on the stairs at the far end of the hall. I didn't catch up with him until he was outside the school and halfway across the football field.

"Give me a break, Jonah," I said, grabbing his arm to stop him from galloping away. I was already panting.

He said something to me that would have earned him a suspension if he had said it to a teacher, jerked his arm away from me, and kept moving. As I kept on his heels, the warning bell sounded behind us. I put on a little speed and got around in front of him.

"I'm sorry," I said.

"Sorry for what? Sorry you said what you said, or just sorry I heard you?"

Both, actually.

"Sorry you're mad at me," I said. He was still plowing forward, and I had to move pretty fast backwards just to keep talking to him. "Come on, Jonah. Cut me some slack here. I thought we were getting to be friends."

"Friends?" The word exploded out of him. "I don't know what you mean by that word, but to me, a friend is a person who is honest with you, not a person who says one thing to your face and something different behind your back."

He was right, of course. I said so.

"I know how you feel," I added.

His face hardened into fury as soon as I had spoken the words, and I knew I had made a big mistake.

"You don't know anything at all about how I feel," he said. "Your father isn't rotting in prison for something he didn't do. Your little brother isn't all messed up from having seen his mother lying dead in the basement of his own house. You don't have people crossing the road to avoid talking to you all the time because they think your dad is some kind of psycho killer. And I'm not talking about strangers, either. I'm talking about people who knew my dad his whole life. People who sat in church beside him, who curled with him or against him every Saturday night for years, people who were friends of his — friends and neighbors. And you didn't lose all the friends you used to have because all of a sudden their parents didn't want them hanging out with someone whose father was in prison. You haven't spent five years of your life with everyone telling you to calm down, get over it, accept reality, when what they really want you to calm down about is the fact that your father is in prison, maybe forever, for something he didn't do. The thing they want you to get over is the injustice of it. The reality they want you to accept is just one big lie. You don't understand. You don't even get it. My father is innocent. How loud do I have to yell that? How many people do I have to say it to? *My dad did not kill my mom.* You got that?"

I had never heard him say so many words all together. I had never heard him explain himself at all.

"Jonah, I'm really sorry — "

"Forget sorry," he said. "Just forget everything, okay? Get out of my way." He shoved me roughly. And hard. I stumbled backwards. He could see I was losing my balance. Then I saw his hand reach out and I was sure he was going to grab my arm and stop me from going down. But he didn't. Instead, he shoved me again, harder this time, and I fell to the ground. As I went down, I felt something give in my ankle. "Stay out of my life," he said. "Leave me alone and don't do me any more favors."

In that moment, as I struggled to a sitting position and watched him stride away, I understood why Ross loathed him the way he did.

"Fine!" I shouted after him. "Fine, run away from the truth, why don't you? Just run and keep on running!"

He didn't even look back. When he was finally out of sight, I picked myself up and limped back to the school. My ankle hurt even more by the time I got there.

Chapter 8

By the time I got back inside the school, I couldn't put any weight on my ankle. I don't think I had ever been more glad to run into a vice-principal, which is what I did almost as soon as I hobbled through one of the back doors. Mr. Moore was standing in the hall. He heard the door click shut and turned in my direction.

"You're late for class," he said.

I tried to take a step and almost fainted from the pain. Mr. Moore hurried toward me.

"Are you all right?" he said.

I shook my head.

He came right up close to me and poked out an elbow.

"Lean on me," he said.

I held his arm tightly and hopped all the way to the school office. I know hopping sounds like fun. It's the kind of thing little kids do when they're playing together. Well, I'll let you in on a little secret. Hopping is harder — and not nearly as much fun as it sounds — when one of your ankles is throbbing.

When we reached the office Mr. Moore sat me down and asked me what had happened. Then he telephoned my mother. Mom called Levesque. Levesque picked me up about ten minutes later and drove me to the hospital where I had the enormous pleasure of sitting on a hard plastic chair in a stuffy little waiting room for two hours before anyone got around to X-raying my ankle. By then it had swelled up to the size of a grapefruit and was throbbing so hard that if I had been alone, I probably would have given myself permission to cry. It hurt so much and I spent so much time biting my lip so that I wouldn't start blubbering like a baby that I didn't believe it when a harried-looking intern told me it wasn't broken. Call me a baby, but I didn't see how anything could hurt that bad and not be fractured. The doctor told me it was sprained — badly sprained. He taped it up, handed me a pair of crutches and said, "Stay off it for a week."

"So," Levesque said after he had helped me into the front seat of the car, "do you want to tell me what happened?"

I fussed with my crutches so that I didn't have to look him in the eye. "I already told you."

"You said you were out on the football field and you fell."

I nodded.

"Mr. Moore told me he met you coming in the back door of the school fifteen minutes after the final bell had rung." He had his police detective voice turned up full force.

"Yeah, and?"

"What were you doing out on the football field after the school bell had sounded?"

"I guess I was running a little behind schedule."

He peered at me a moment before he said, "How did you *fall?*"

I didn't like the little spike of emphasis he put on the last word.

"I was hurrying, so I wouldn't be late."

"You were already late."

"I didn't want to be later."

"So you're saying you were hurrying back into the school and you fell?"

"Right."

"Did you trip over something?"

"I guess."

"What did you trip over?"

"I don't know. A stone, a stick, an uneven patch of ground."

"So you tripped on something and fell and sprained your ankle?"

I nodded.

"You're sure?"

"Sure I'm sure. I was there."

He peered at me again, then he turned the key in the ignition, drove me home and set me up with an ice pack and a couple of Tylenols before going back to work.

The whole time I'd been sitting in the hospital waiting room, my ankle throbbing, I was mad at Jonah. He pushed me. He did it hard and he did it on purpose. He had meant to hurt me. I was still mad when I got home. I was being subjected to a week on crutches, thanks to some guy with a bad temper who had decided to take his problems out on me. I was not thinking kind thoughts about Jonah Shackleton.

Then the Tylenol and the ice pack started to take

the edge off my pain, and I found myself wondering what it must be like to be ten-going-on-eleven years old with a mother just murdered and a father convicted of having done it. I wondered about losing all your friends and feeling like everyone you had ever known had turned against you. And then I wondered about making a new friend and feeling like that friend had turned against you, too. I felt pretty bad. I also felt hungry, so I grabbed the crutches that were propped up by the side of my bed and hobbled — and almost toppled — down the stairs. Nice one, Chloe. Keep that up and you'll get your broken ankle after all.

As soon as I reached the kitchen, Shendor started to bark on the other side of the door to the basement. We had decided on Shendor as a kind of joke. She was a big golden dog. *Un chien d'or,* Levesque had said. *Chien d'or,* Shendor. I thought it sounded pretty good. I didn't know much about dogs, but I couldn't help feeling sorry for her. First she had been abandoned. Then she got stuck in a gloomy old basement while everyone was at work or at school. I hobbled over to the door and opened it. Not my smartest-ever move because Shendor almost bowled me over in her rush to thank me. It took nearly five minutes to calm her down enough so that I could do what I had come down here to do — get something to eat.

I decided to start with a big glass of cold milk.

Trying to carry a container of milk from the fridge to the counter while limping with crutches was — big surprise! — not as easy as it sounds.

The milk was in one of those big plastic gallon jugs that, when they're full, are as heavy as a small child. The weight tipped me to one side and I lost my balance. When I tried to get a better grip on my crutch, the darned thing slipped from my hand. I bet you think those plastic jugs are spill-proof. Maybe they are — when they're not cracked after having crashed to the floor. Milk was seeping out all over the tiles. Great. Just what I needed — a whole new set of challenges. Hunt under the sink for rags, get down on the floor to mop up the mess that Shendor hadn't already lapped up (fantastic, there was dog slobber *and* milk all over the floor), struggle up again — after another battle with my crutches — with the leaky milk jug, transfer the milk to a couple of pots — I couldn't find anything else. By the time I had the pots in the fridge, I had lost my appetite, and the last thing I wanted to think about was milk. My ankle was throbbing again, too, from all the up-and-down I had subjected it to. I headed for the living room and the TV. Shendor padded in behind me.

To get to the living room, I had to pass the door to the basement. It was ajar, and I pushed it open. Shendor must have thought I was going to shoo her down there, because she bounded out of the room. But I wasn't interested in her. I was interested in the basement. I had been down there a half-dozen times since I had heard about Mary Shackleton, looking around and seeing nothing helpful.

The stairs leading to our unfinished basement were wooden. The floor at the bottom was gray painted concrete. I stood at the top now, wobbling on my crutches, and stared into the gloom. What if I came home and found my mother lying down there, dead? What if everyone tried to convince me that Levesque had done it? I was one hundred percent convinced that you couldn't make Levesque commit murder, even if you put a gun to his head. But what if he caught a bad break, like Donald Marshall or David Milgaard, and what if, despite what I knew in my heart to be true, he was convicted? How would I feel? What would I do? Wouldn't I want to take a swing at the tenth and the hundredth and the millionth person who made a crack about what he had supposedly done?

The thing is, though, that if a guy like Levesque ever decided to cross the line, he would be smart about it. For one thing, he'd make sure he had a decent alibi. For another, he'd probably try to make the whole thing look like an accident. If you shoved someone down those stairs hard enough and they landed head first on the concrete floor, you could probably kill her and claim it was an accident. But to whack the person over the head first and then shove them? That just wasn't good planning. But maybe, like the newspapers had said, Harold Shackleton wasn't very bright. I had never met him. I had no idea whether he was one of the sharpest knives in the drawer or one of the dullest.

* * *

The next day Levesque drove me to school and picked me up again afterwards. At school, Ross was my guardian angel. When he offered to carry my books from class to locker to class, I thought he was kidding — we weren't in any of the same classes. So I was surprised — and a little touched — when I found him waiting breathless at the door of Ms. Pileggi's math class to fetch and carry for me.

"I thought you had Spanish last period," I said.

He nodded and gasped for breath.

"But Mr. Azoulay's class is in the new wing, on the third floor," I said. The class I had just finished was on the first floor of the old wing — which made the two classrooms about as far apart as it was possible to be.

He nodded again and managed to pant, "No problem."

"Maybe you should go out for track," I said.

He looked pleased.

On Monday, when I was supposed to tutor Jonah, I asked Levesque to pick me up a little later than usual. When Ross gathered up my books at the end of the day, I said, "Do you mind putting those in my locker for me? I have to do something."

He nodded and I knew from the look on his face that he wanted to ask what that something was, but he didn't. He headed for my locker. I headed for the library on the third floor.

Jonah didn't show up.

I know he was in school — I had seen him. I had seen him dozens of times, at the far end of the hall or at the bottom of a flight of stairs or disappearing around a corner. He was avoiding me and we both knew it. So why did I hobble up those two flights to the library, only to have to turn around and hobble right back down again and then sit around for an hour to wait for Levesque? Pure stubbornness, I guess. But even pure stubbornness loses its edge after a while.

* * *

Two days later, when I faced those stairs, I hesitated. I stood at the bottom, craning my neck to look way up, and argued with myself about what to do. My ankle was feeling a lot better. I had seen the doctor who had taped it up and he had told me I should be able to walk without crutches in another two days. But that didn't mean I wanted to go up those stairs again today. It just wasn't worth it.

"I know how you feel," said a voice behind me. "Seems like a lot of effort for nothing, right?"

I had become pretty proficient on my crutches, but turning was still tricky. It took a few moments for me to maneuver the one hundred and eighty degrees. While I did, I thought about what I wanted to say — thanks for introducing me to the crutch experience . . . Thanks for being such a jerk . . . You're lucky I didn't have you charged with assault . . . Get out of my face, you miserable thug. But when I was finally face-to-face with Jonah, I didn't say any of those things. I didn't have time, because he said,

"I'm sorry."

I stared at him and waited for more.

"I'm sorry I shoved you," he said, "and I'm sorry you hurt yourself — "

"*I* hurt myself?"

He hung his head a little. "I'm sorry I hurt you. I lost my temper. That's not an excuse. I'm supposed to know better than that. I just — " He looked directly at me with those blue, blue eyes. "I'm sorry," he repeated. "It won't happen again."

"Okay," I said.

He stared at me as if I had just offered him a million dollars and he was looking for the trick, the catch. But there was no catch. He had hurt me and he had apologized and it had sounded sincere. You couldn't ask for more than that, could you? You couldn't ask that he undo the past.

"You want to do some French?" I asked.

"I can't today. I have to pick up Jay at school."

"So, pick him up and meet me somewhere. We're behind schedule. Madame Benoit won't be happy about that."

He studied me hard again. "I don't get you," he said.

"That makes us even. I don't get you, either," I said. "But as far as I know, you still need French tutoring and I can still help you with that. So how about it?"

"We could go to Stella's," he suggested. Stella's Famous Home Cooking. "Aunt Linda won't mind if we sit in one of the back booths." Then he looked at my foot and my crutches. "Maybe that's not such a great idea," he said. "It's pretty far."

"That's not a problem," I said. "If you carry my books, I can manage. I'm pretty good on these things."

He smiled. Jonah Shackleton smiled at me for the second time since I had met him. "Okay," he said.

To be honest, my armpits hurt by the time we reached Stella's. Armpits, if you ask me, are the main problem with crutches. But I didn't complain because I didn't want Jonah to feel bad.

Aunt Linda was standing at the cash register when Jonah opened the door to Stella's. She looked up as Jay scrambled into the restaurant ahead of me. Then I limped in, followed by Jonah, who was carrying my books. She peered at Jonah. Her face formed a question I didn't understand. I don't know what kind of look Jonah gave her in return or what she managed to read on his face, but all of a sudden she smiled. It made her look a lot younger. She brought sodas for Jonah and me, and ice cream for Jay, and then she hovered a moment to smooth Jay's hair with her fingers.

We studied French for a solid hour while Jay sat at Jonah's side, turning the pages of a book, his finger traveling across the page, his lips moving as he silently formed words. He didn't close his book until Jonah closed his binder. When Jonah reached for his backpack, so did Jay. Their movements were in perfect synch as they put away their things. Then they got up together to get their jackets from a hook along the back wall. Aunt Linda, pulling a coat on over her uniform, came over to me and said, "You'd better let me drive you home."

I started to protest — I didn't want her taking time off work on my account when I could call home for a ride — but she wouldn't listen. "Where do you live?" she asked. A strange look appeared on her face when I told her, but she didn't say anything. She handed me my coat and carried my backpack for me. We all went outside and piled into her tired old Chev', Aunt Linda and Jay in the front, Jonah and I in the back.

The sun was pretty much down as we glided along Centre Street and headed down one of East Hastings' paved residential avenues. Properties in East Hastings were huge compared to those in Montreal. The houses were bigger, too, and much farther apart. And the farther you got away from the center of town, the more spaced out the houses became until, by the time you got to the street where I lived — which was gravel, not paved — the properties were enormous. A lot of them were wooded. Ours was, at the back — lawn sloping down until it hit scrub, then bush. Once, during the summer, I had looked out my window and seen a deer at the edge of the property and I remember thinking to myself, "We're not in Kansas any more, Toto."

Our house is on a little rise, which means you get a good view of the front of it after dark, when the lights are on. As we approached it, I glanced over at Jonah. He was leaning forward in his seat, staring intently ahead. So was Jay. There was a strange silence in the car. I peered up at Aunt Linda. The smile had slipped from her face. It took a moment before I understood what was going on. Oh, no. When I'd given her the address, *she* realized she'd be driving me to Jonah's old house, but *he* had no idea where I lived. And here we were pulling up to our house — which had been his and Jay's house. The place where their mother had been murdered. I wondered when they had last been in it, or even been near it. All of a sudden I wished I hadn't accepted Aunt Linda's offer of a ride.

The car turned up the driveway and slid to a stop in front of the house. Before I could open the door on my side, Jonah had jumped out and was circling around the back of the car. He opened the door for me and reached in to help me out. I let him. What else could I do? But when he started to walk me to the house, I said, "It's okay. I can manage."

He nodded. I glanced back at the car and saw Jay's face pressed up against the passenger side window. He was peering wide-eyed at the house. I wondered how much he remembered of that terrible day. I wondered if he went with Jonah once a month to see his father. I wondered what it was like when your only parental contact was in a prison visiting room, watched by armed guards, and when it looked like it would stay that way until you were grown up with children of your own. "Jonah?" I had to say something. I felt bad about what he had heard me saying to Ross. I felt bad about making him come here. I felt worse about Jay. "Jonah, I'm sorry — about everything."

He looked up at the house for a moment. I could only imagine what he was thinking.

"I'm going to do what you said," he told me. "I'm going to find out who killed my mother. At least, I'm going to try." He looked at me. "I could use a little help, though, if you're still interested," he said. "It doesn't even matter to me if you do it because you want to show me I'm wrong." He looked up at the house again. "Maybe you're right. Maybe I am crazy to believe in my father. No one else does. But I have to know. One way or another, I have to know for myself who killed my mother. So what do you think?" He peered at me in the faint light from the porch. "Will you help me?"

I glanced back at the small, pale face in the front of the car. Then I nodded.

Chapter 9

There are only three ways to get around in East Hastings. Well, four, if you happen to own a horse, which I don't. Up here, you can walk from where you are to where you want to be. You can take the bus, assuming there's a bus that runs between point A where you're standing and point B where you'd like to be standing, and assuming it's the right time of day, or the right day of the week, to catch that bus. Or you can do what pretty well everyone does — you can get to your destination in your own vehicle: car, van, truck, motorcycle, ATV, snowmobile (depending on the season, of course).

Chartoff Hauling was twelve miles out of town on Municipal Sideroad Number Nine. Bob Chartoff's house sat on a piece of land another three miles farther down the same road. Kinsey Automotive Parts, where Fred Simla was a vice-president, was a full hour away, over in Elder Bay. Fred Simla lived halfway between East Hastings and his place of work. Norman Himmel lived and worked in Morrisville, forty-five minutes north of East Hastings. If we were going to get to all of those places and talk to all three men, we needed transportation.

Mom and Levesque have a car. They also have jobs that keep them busy. And even if they were free, they would have asked a million questions apiece before agreeing to take us where we wanted to go — assuming they agreed at all. Same problem, only more so, with Jonah's Aunt Linda. And since neither Jonah nor I had learner's permits, let alone driver's licenses, we couldn't even borrow a car to get where we needed to go.

"We have to find someone who won't mind driving us," I said to Jonah the next day at lunch, my first day off crutches, for which my armpits were grateful. I felt a little twinge in my ankle with each step I took, but so far, so good.

"We have to find someone who won't mind driving us and won't mind having me in their car," Jonah said. "This is going to sound lame, considering that I've lived here all my life and you're new in town, but I don't have any ideas."

I did.

* * *

"I'll pay for your gas," I told Ross.

"No."

"I'll throw in a car wash — "

"No."

"And dinner. You do this, Ross, and I'll take you out for a nice dinner."

He hesitated a moment.

"Okay, I'll drive you," he said. "But Shackleton doesn't get near my car, let alone in it."

"Jonah has to come with us. We're doing this for him."

"*We?*"

"He's not as bad as you think."

He rubbed his jaw rather pointedly.

"There could be a story in this, Ross. If Jonah turns out to be right about his father, your newspaper can be the first to break the news."

"First of all, it's not *my* newspaper — "

"You're the editor."

"And second, there's no way that Shackleton is right. What's the matter with you, Chloe? Last I heard, you were doing this as a reality check for the guy. Now you sound as if you actually believe his delusions. Or is there something else going on?"

I didn't like his tone of voice all of a sudden. "What do you mean by that?"

"Nothing." He looked at his computer screen. It was an annoying habit of his. Want to avoid an argument? Stare at your stupid computer. It made me want to reach over and hit Exit. *Without* saving whatever he had been working on.

"What are you trying to say, Ross?"

"I'll do it," he said. I doubt he could have sounded less thrilled about the prospect.

"Never mind."

"I said, I'll do it."

Maybe it was a case of too little, too late, but I said, "I'm not sure I want you to."

"Who else are you going to get? It's not like the whole town is clamoring to be Jonah Shackleton's chauffeur."

"Oh, I see. So you think you can be as snide as you want because you've got me over a barrel — I have to go with you or not go at all. Well, I've got news for you. I'll walk the sixty miles to Elder Bay before I accept a ride with you."

We glared at each other for a few moments, then I turned to leave. The next thing I knew, he had slipped around in front of me to block my way.

"I'm sorry," he said. "Look, I'll do it and I won't grumble about it, okay?"

"You don't have to."

"Geez, Chloe, do you really want me to withdraw the offer? I'm going to say this one last time, and then I'm going to take you at your word. I am officially offering to drive you and Shackleton wherever you want to go — in return for gas money and a really nice dinner. That's a dinner for two, by the way, not three — you and me, no Shackleton. This offer is valid for a limited time only. Say no one more time, Chloe, and that's it."

"Okay," I said. "Okay, thanks, Ross. I really appreciate this." I leaned over and kissed him lightly on the cheek. His hand flew to his face to touch the place where I had kissed him. "Meet us right after school, okay? We'll go see Bob Chartoff."

I sat up front with Ross. Jonah sat in the back seat. For the first few miles, no one said anything. Finally, I couldn't stand it anymore. I decided to dive in, despite the chill.

"Do you know Bob Chartoff, Jonah?"

"No." At least, I think he said no. Maybe he just grunted.

"Your dad never talked about him?"

Another "no" grunt.

"You don't remember seeing him around your house, do you?"

"I don't even know what he looks like," Jonah said.

"Because if he had ever been at your house — "

"Chloe, he said he didn't know the guy," Ross said. "Give him a break. He was ten years old at the time."

I looked at Ross when he said that and saw something change in his face. It was as if he were thinking it over — really thinking. He glanced in the rearview mirror at Jonah, and suddenly he didn't seem so angry to have him in the car. Maybe they were bonding or something. That would be good. Or maybe they weren't. Whatever had happened, we rode the rest of the way in silence.

Chartoff Hauling consisted of a long, curved-roof metal building, the kind that looks like a log half-buried in the ground. It was surrounded by an expanse of gravel, marked off by a six-foot-high chain-link fence that, frankly, I didn't see the reason for. What was there to steal, except maybe a bunch of garbage trucks that probably parked there at the end of the day?

The gate was open, so we had no problem getting in.

"The place looks deserted," Ross said as he shut off the engine. He sounded almost relieved.

"If it was deserted, the gate would be locked," I pointed out. "Come on." Anybody watching us would have noticed that I was the one who led the way. They would also have noticed that Ross hung back behind Jonah.

I knocked on the door, but got no answer.

"What did I tell you?" Ross said. "Nobody's home." He turned quickly back to the car. I don't think I was imagining the little pirouette of relief in his movement.

I twisted the doorknob. It gave and the door swung open.

"What did you tell me?" I asked. Actually, it came out more like a taunt.

Ross turned back more slowly. He didn't look carefree any more.

"Are you coming or what?" I asked as I pushed my way into the building.

A guy who looked about twenty was sitting in front of a computer, entering a bunch of information from a stack of papers in front of him. He glanced up when we came in, but didn't say anything.

"Is Mr. Chartoff here?" I asked.

The guy turned toward the office door behind him and called, "Dad? There's some kids here who want to talk to you." Then he went back to his work.

A moment later, the door behind him opened and a big man appeared. When I say big, I don't mean fat. I mean huge. Tall, for one thing. His head seemed to scrape the top of the doorframe. And wide. I was half expecting him to have to swing sideways to get out of his office. He didn't, though.

"What do you kids want?"

"Mr. Chartoff? My name's Chloe Yan. These are my friends — "

"Selling something for your school, huh?" Bob

Chartoff said. "What is it this time? Chocolate bars?" He looked us over for cartons of chocolate and seemed disappointed that we weren't carrying any. "Raffle tickets? Well, come on in and I'll see what I can do. Support your local school, I always say. Isn't that right, Mel?"

The guy at the desk rolled his eyes. "Whatever."

Bob Chartoff ignored him. "Well, come on," he said to us.

When you see your opportunity, you have to take it. I scurried into his office. Ross and Jonah followed with less enthusiasm. I felt like I was leading troops who would much rather have been retreating from battle.

Mr. Chartoff sat down at his desk and yanked open a drawer. He pulled one of those big company checkbooks from it and looked expectantly at me.

"Well, give me your pitch."

"Actually, we didn't come to pitch you anything," I said. "We just wanted to ask you a few questions for an article we're writing for the school newspaper."

He closed his checkbook and leaned back in his chair. It squealed in protest.

"School newspaper, huh?" He seemed pleased. "What's the article about? Local businessmen? Local businesses? I'd be pleased to tell you whatever you want to know." He stood up, walked to the window and pulled aside the blind so that he could look out. "There she is," he said. "My business. Yes, you heard me, I said business. A lot of people don't think of hauling garbage as a real business. They say, what's the big deal, Bob, it's not as if it's General Motors or Microsoft. They think garbage disposal is the kind of thing any half-wit can do. They don't realize how much know-how and planning it takes. But think about it a minute. Where would this town be without someone to take away the waste? How'd you all like to be living on a mountain of refuse? Not a pleasant thought, is it? Well, who's going to haul that refuse away? And where are they going to put it? And how are they going to make sure that when it's dumped, it doesn't cause problems? Let me tell you — "

"Actually, Mr. Chartoff," I said — I hated to interrupt him, and I sure hated to tell him that we weren't interested in his business, but — "the article we're working on has to do with the North Mines Landfill project."

"The landfill project?" Mr. Chartoff leaned forward and I suddenly felt like I was standing in the shadow of the Leaning Tower of Pisa. I hoped he wouldn't topple over onto me. "For the school newspaper, you say?"

I nodded.

"The East Hastings school newspaper?"

I nodded again.

His big face clouded. "Didn't I hear something about some clown at the high school writing an editorial against the project last year? The tree huggers got hold of that piece and started making a big stink down south again. Something to the effect that the future generation of East Hastings didn't want their water poisoned by trash from down south, as I recall." It didn't sound like a pleasant recollection. "That wasn't you, was it?" He peered sternly at me.

"That was Ross," I said, and nodded toward him.

Ross shot me an I'll-get-you-if-it's-the-last-thing-I-ever-do look. I don't know why he was so mad. If he believed what he had written, then he should stand by it. Besides, if I were him and I had written it and it had made such a big splash, I would have been proud.

"And this," I said to Mr. Chartoff, "is Jonah Shackleton."

"Shackleton?" Mr. Chartoff frowned. "Not related to Harold Shackleton, are you?"

"He's my dad," Jonah said. He pulled himself up tall when he said it.

"You don't say," Mr. Chartoff said. He sank onto his chair. "How about that?"

"Do you know Harold Shackleton, Mr. Chartoff?" I asked.

"I can't really say I know him. Seen him around, of course. And then there was the trial. But do I know him as in, did I ever shake hands with the man?" He shook his head. "Look, if you kids are here because you're planning to try and rile things up again in cahoots with those tree huggers, you should give it some more thought. Jobs were hard to come by up here five years ago and they've only gotten more scarce since then. If you write another one of those articles and throw in your lot with those environmental yahoos who are trying to put the brakes on the landfill project

113

this time, people won't be too happy with you."

I opened my mouth to say that wasn't what we were here for, but changed my mind at the last minute.

"So are we going to have to put you down as a no comment for our article?" I said instead.

"You can put me down as whatever you want," he said. "I don't have any stake in the deal. But I can tell you this. The politicians down at Queen's Park can't afford to nitpick about non-existent environmental problems up here any more. Not when they've got a great big environmental problem right in their own backyard. Toronto is running out of places to dump its trash. Even the folks down south who were against the project five years ago aren't putting up much of a fight this time. You think they want to be up to their eyeballs in their own rubbish? And folks up here? Folks up here want jobs. I'm only sorry I sold out when I did."

Ross was the first one to speak. He said, "So, what you're telling us is that the North Mines project is going ahead again." He pulled out a notebook.

Mr. Chartoff's eyes grew small in his big round face. "Say, what's this all about? You kids come into my office on the pretext that you're selling raffle tickets — "

"We never said we were selling anything," I pointed out. Then, before he could speak again, I said, "What did you mean when you said you're sorry you sold out when you did? Aren't you still involved in the project?"

114

He shook his head. "I haven't been involved for years. When Mary Shackleton decided not to sell the land, that was the end of the road for me. I pulled out."

"So the project *is* going ahead again?" Ross repeated.

Mr. Chartoff looked annoyed.

"But you were part of the group of businessmen who offered Mary Shackleton a lot of money for her land, weren't you?" I said.

"Are you asking me or telling me?" Mr. Chartoff said. I guess he was mad at himself for letting something slip that maybe he shouldn't have. I would have been willing to bet anything that the decision to resurrect the project wasn't public knowledge yet.

"You must have been pretty upset when Mrs. Shackleton turned you down," I said.

Mr. Chartoff's chair crackled and groaned as he settled back into it. "I'll admit to disappointment," he said. "That landfill project was a fine opportunity. We had already invested a lot of money in the plans and the environmental assessment, all on the strength of a verbal agreement with Claude LaCasse that he'd sell the land once we got the all-clear. Then he died." He paused to look again at Jonah. "I was sorry to see your granddad pass," he said, "and not just because of our business together. He was a great guy, old Claude. So sure, when Mary Shackleton refused to make good on her dad's promise to sell, I was disappointed. But upset? Not me."

"Even though you had spent money on the deal?" I asked.

He shrugged. "Business is business. Sometimes you gamble a little, and sometimes when you do, you lose. It didn't hurt me much, though. I'm doing well enough with this business, thank you very much, and I have other interests. I wasn't the one with the big dreams of breaking free, of jumping off the treadmill of wage slavery. I'm a free man, my own boss. Always have been and I plan to keep it that way, North Mines Landfill project or not."

Maybe he was telling the truth. Maybe he wasn't. How did cops figure these things out?

"How about your partners? Did they feel the same way?"

He looked at me for a moment and then shook his head. "You really are something, you know that?" he said. "Bunch of kids, walking right in here and asking me all these questions."

"About your partners, Mr. Chartoff," I prompted.

For a moment I thought he was going to laugh. He didn't, though.

"Did they take the bad news as calmly as I did?" he said. "No, they did not. When Mary Shackleton reneged on our deal with her father, it made them pretty angry. Being involved in that project was like riding a seesaw. First it seemed like a great idea, smooth sailing. Then we lost old Claude and Mary refused to sell. She was pretty determined, so I bailed out. The other partners bought me out a couple of days before . . . " He glanced again at Jonah. "Afterwards, when Harold sold the land, it looked like a go again. Then those tree huggers down south kicked up such a fuss that the politicians got scared and put a halt to the project, which meant a lot of people were out a lot of money for a lot of useless land."

I pondered what he had said. If Bob Chartoff had sold his share of the project before Mary Shackleton died, then he didn't have much of a motive for murder.

"What about Mr. Simla and Mr. Himmel?" I said. "How upset were they when Mary Shackleton refused to sell?"

"Simla and Himmel are sled dogs," he said, "if you know what I mean."

"Uh, well . . . " I hated to admit it but, no, I didn't.

"In a dogsled team," he explained, "unless you're the lead dog, the scenery never changes, it's the same grind day after day. Simla and Himmel were — are — strictly middle management. They aren't the head honcho, they report to the head honcho. You know, a couple of guys with big dreams and no way to get to that top rung of the ladder — until that landfill project came along. They saw that project as their ticket to something bigger. So how were they when Mary Shackleton refused to sell her land? Pretty darned upset, I'd say." He peered at me. "I'm not sure where you're going with this, though."

"Actually, Mr. Chartoff," I said, and took a deep breath, "we think Harold Shackleton may be innocent."

Bob Chartoff's reaction was like a minor explosion — of laughter. He guffawed heartily. Then his eyes met Jonah's and suddenly he looked ashamed of himself.

"Sorry, son. That was rude of me. If I hurt your feelings in any way, I apologize. I didn't mean to. It's just that, well, I don't know how else to say it except straight out — your father had his day in court and a jury delivered its verdict."

If we were going to do this, it was a sure bet we were going to run into this reaction. I figured we might as well get used to it. We might as well learn to deal with it.

"That's okay," I said. I swear I could feel Jonah's eyes drilling into the back of my neck. I would have been willing to bet it wasn't okay with him. "I'm sure you're not the only person who thinks we're crazy to think he's innocent. But, look, if it was my dad in prison, I'd want to be sure he was the right guy. Wouldn't you?"

"Well, sure, but — "

"So we thought we'd look into it. Ask some questions. Check the facts. Thanks for your time, Mr. Chartoff," I said.

He grinned at me. "Sherlock Holmes," he said. "I know he was a man and he was English and he had a doctor for a sidekick, but I like those stories. I read every single one of them when I was about your age."

I wasn't sure what to say to that, so I thanked him for his time again.

"Now what?" Ross asked as we piled back into the car.

"Now we go see Fred Simla."

"Now?"

I checked my watch. It was getting late.

"Okay, so tomorrow we go see Fred Simla."

Chapter 10

Levesque was home for dinner that night. As he buried his fork in the mound of mashed potatoes on his plate, he looked across the table at me and said, "What did you do after school today, Chloe?"

You have to react fast when he springs a question like that on you. At least, you do if you want to keep your private life private. You have to resist the urge to duck your head down to your own plate or to look away — doing either of those things makes it seem like you have something to hide. Instead, you have to look him square in the eye. I've found that it helps if you make yourself think about a totally different topic at the same time — so when I looked at him, I thought about tomorrow's history test, not about Jonah Shackleton. I didn't have anything to hide about history, so there was nothing for him to read in my eyes.

"Today?" I said. "Nothing special. Why?"

My mother looked like a spectator at a tennis match. Her head swiveled from Levesque to me and back again. I guess she figured something was up. So did Phoebe, because she was grinning the way she always did when I was about to land feet first in trouble. If I'd had to put money on it, I would have bet that Levesque was just fishing, although I couldn't figure out why.

He reached for the salt shaker.

"I got a call today from a fellow named Bob Chartoff," he said to my mother.

Okay, so I would have lost whatever I had bet. He wasn't fishing.

"Chartoff?" my mother said. "Why is that name so familiar?"

"Because it's painted on the side of all the garbage trucks up here," Phoebe said.

My mother looked perplexed. "Why would a garbage collector call you?" she said.

Levesque listened carefully to my mother's question, then turned to me for the answer.

"What makes you think I know?" I said.

"Because he called about you," Levesque said.

"Oh, dear," my mother said. "Now what have you done?"

"Yeah," Phoebe said, grinning, "*now* what have you done?"

Nothing like family solidarity.

"Nothing!" I said.

They obviously didn't believe me because they both looked at Levesque, to see what he was going to say.

"Bob Chartoff wanted to know if the police are re-opening their investigation of the Mary Shackleton murder case."

"Why would he think that?" my mother said.

"It seems that a certain Chloe Yan visited him today, along with two friends, one of whom was Jonah Shackleton — "

Phoebe hooted. "Chloe's in trouble!"

"Shut up," I hissed.

"Chloe!" my mother said. It was hard to tell whether she was angry because of Chartoff or because I had told Phoebe to shut up. Mom didn't approve of such sisterly talk.

I ignored them both and looked directly at Levesque. "I don't know what he was complaining about. It wasn't as if we were harassing him or anything. We just asked him a few questions, which, by the way, he seemed more than happy to answer. We didn't do anything illegal."

"He didn't say he had been harassed," Levesque said. "If anything, he seemed amused."

"So what's the problem?" I said.

"The problem is, I don't want you making trouble, especially if it ends up getting associated with the police department or me. Police work is serious. It's not a game. Do you understand?"

I felt like someone had jammed my finger into an electrical outlet. Something was wrong. Something was very wrong. My mother picked up on it right away. She peered at Levesque, a look of concern on her face. Levesque wasn't the kind of guy who worried about trouble. If anything, he was the kind of guy who stirred it up.

"I haven't done anything wrong," I said again.

"Well, see that you don't."

I made a sour face.

"I mean it, Chloe," he said. "You keep your nose clean."

He said it the way a high school principal would after he caught you spiking drinks at a school dance and decided, oh so generously, to give you a second chance. It made me angry.

"I didn't do anything wrong," I said again. Everyone just stared at me with a "yeah, sure" look on their faces. Which made even me angrier. I downed cutlery and left the table.

* * *

Some people, when they're told point-blank not to do something, comply. Other people interpret an order to cease and desist as an invitation to keep right on going, sometimes with even more determination. I tend to be the second kind of person. I don't like anyone telling me what I can and can't do.

We had agreed to meet right after school on Friday. Ross was already in the parking lot when I got there. Jonah wasn't. As we waited for him, it occurred to me that I hadn't seen Jonah in the cafeteria at lunchtime. In fact, I hadn't seen him anytime during the day. I could only shrug when Ross asked me where he was. We leaned against Ross's mother's car and waited ten minutes, then ten minutes more. Then Ross glanced at his watch.

"So, what do you think? You think he bailed out on you?" he asked. I noticed right away that he had said "on you," not "on us."

I didn't answer. A few more minutes passed before Ross said, "What do you want to do?"

I was just about to say, "Let's go look for him," when I saw Jonah hurrying across the parking lot toward us. Jay was clinging to his hand.

"Sorry," Jonah said to me. He didn't even glance

at Ross. "I'm really sorry." There were dark circles under his eyes. He looked as if he hadn't slept in years.

"Are we going or what?" Ross said.

"I can't," Jonah said.

Ross reacted as if Jonah had just spit on him. "Hey, we're doing this for you, you know."

Jonah ignored him. He knelt down and held Jay firmly by the shoulders. "I need to talk to Chloe, okay?" he said. "I'm just going to step over there for a minute. I won't go away. I promise."

Jay didn't move. He didn't nod. He just stared at Jonah with big dark eyes. He looked as if he hadn't slept for a while, either, but he stayed where Jonah had put him. Jonah straightened up and led me a few paces away from the car.

"I have to drop this whole thing," he said.

"What?"

"I have to drop it. It's not good for Jay."

"But, Jonah — "

"I think maybe all that protest stuff was a mistake. The media coverage, the run-ins with McDermott. I think maybe that's what did it." He cast a worried glance back at Jay.

"Did what?" I asked. I was completely lost. "Jonah, you said you wanted to clear your dad. You said — "

"He's been having trouble in school. A teacher got mad at him because he wasn't paying attention and he just got up and walked out of the class. It turned out he walked right out of the school. We didn't know where he was, for *hours.*"

He glanced over at Jay, as if to reassure himself that the little guy was still there.

"He's having nightmares again," Jonah continued. "A couple of days ago he started wetting his bed again, too. Then last night — " He looked at Jay again, then led me a few paces farther away from where Jay was standing. "I was sound asleep. Then I heard screaming. I don't mean just yelling, either. I mean screaming. Blood-curdling slasher-movie screaming." His eyes were wide with the memory of what he was telling me. "At first I couldn't figure out where it was coming from. I got out of bed. Aunt Linda was out in the hall. She looked terrified. I guess I was too. Anyway, we followed the noise. I had my baseball bat in my hand." He shook his head. "Geez, what was I thinking? That I was going to find some burglar screaming his head off downstairs?" He looked at me with his blue, blue eyes. "It was Jay," he said. "We found him in the basement, screaming. I guess he'd been sleepwalking. It took nearly an hour to calm him down. Aunt Linda was pretty spooked. I can't do this anymore, Chloe, not if it's going to do this to Jay. Not if it's going to make him the way he was after — after Mom died. Sorry."

Sorry? He was apologizing to me, like this was more important to me than it was to him. How had I ever, even for a minute, thought that Jonah Shackleton was some kind of creep? I watched him walk back to Jay. I watched him take Jay's hand in his own. I watched him duck down and whisper something into the little boy's ear, something that

125

must have been reassuring because when Jay looked back up at him, there was a look of relief in his eyes. Then I watched them walk out of the parking lot together.

"What was that all about?" Ross asked.

I filled him in.

"So I guess that's that, huh?" he said when I had finished.

Ross didn't know me well yet.

* * *

The second shift had punched in and was working its way up to its first coffee break at Kinsey Automotive Parts by the time Ross and I pulled up in front of the low sprawling building. I checked my watch — a quarter to five.

"Maybe he's gone for the day," Ross said.

"Maybe," I said. There was one way to find out. I reached for the car door. Ross put a hand on my arm to hold me back.

"You're not *really* going to do this again, are you?" he asked.

"Do what?"

"March in there and ask all those questions about the landfill project. Geez, why don't you just come right out with the big questions? Excuse me, Mr. Simla, but would you mind accounting for your whereabouts on a certain morning five years ago? Or, excuse me, but we were just wondering — did you kill Mary Shackleton?"

"I guess we could ask him both those questions." I meant it as a joke, but Ross didn't laugh. He didn't even crack a smile. "What's wrong?" I asked

"This is ridiculous."

"You didn't think it was ridiculous when we went to see Bob Chartoff."

He gave me an odd look, and suddenly I got it. He had been awfully relieved when it looked as if Chartoff Hauling was locked. He had thought it was ridiculous. He hadn't wanted to be there.

"You're still convinced Harold Shackleton did it, right?"

"You're starting to sound like you think he didn't. You said this was all about helping Jonah see that his father is in prison for a reason. It doesn't sound that way now."

I stared at him. I wasn't sure what I thought anymore. Ross was right. I had started this to help Jonah come to terms with what had happened. Somewhere along the line, though, everything had changed. I found myself wanting to make things different. I found myself wanting to prove that Jonah was right, that the police had somehow made a mistake, that they'd got the wrong man. That would help Jonah more than anything else possibly could. It would give Jay back his dad and maybe put an end to his nightmares. It would put back together a family that had been torn apart so violently. I looked at Ross. He was probably right. What I was doing was probably crazy. But I couldn't walk away, not without trying.

"Okay, look, I appreciate the lift," I said. "You can wait for me out here if you want. It's okay."

Ross thought about it for a moment, and I was pretty sure he was going to accept the offer.

Instead he grumbled, threw up his arms in disgust, and pushed open the car door. As I opened the door on my side I heard him say, "I must be crazy. I must be right out of my mind." Maybe he was, but he followed me into the building.

First we had to deal with a security guard.

"We'd like to see Mr. Simla, please," I said.

The security guard, true to his occupation, didn't budge. It didn't surprise me. I don't think too highly of security guards. Especially young ones, like the guy who was standing between me and access to Fred Simla. There he was, a good head and shoulders taller than me, swaggering in his uniform, thinking he was some kind of big deal when in actual fact he was just one more guy who hadn't made it into the police academy but who, I bet you a million dollars, had it in his mind that some day he was going to be a cop or a P.I. or something equally exciting. Right now, though, and probably forever, he was a big yawn. Worse, he was an obstacle who was acting more important than he really was and who got his kicks by bullying everyone in his path because, hey, he was wearing a uniform and we weren't.

"What's your business with Mr. Simla?" this security guard said.

I looked him straight in the eye — make like a princess, Chloe, make him understand that you occupy a higher plane of existence than he does — and said, "Do us both a favor and just tell him Chloe is here, would you?"

He blinked. He looked hard at me. I didn't blink.

Then he turned, punched in a code on the little keypad on the door, and went inside, leaving us standing in the foyer.

"Just tell him Chloe is here?" Ross hissed behind me. "What's that all about?"

It was all about pretending you belong. If you do it well enough, people will go along with it, at least for a while.

A moment later the guard was back, accompanied by a balding man in a middle management suit who I assumed was Fred Simla. I plastered a smile on my face and waved vigorously at him. He seemed startled.

"Hi, Mr. Simla," I said, when the guard pushed open the door to let him through.

Fred Simla stared at me. "Do I know you?"

"Chloe Yan," I said. I thrust out my hand. He hesitated but, being an adult — and a vice-president — he took it and we shook. "And this is my friend Ross Jenkins. We're with the *East Hastings Herald.*"

He frowned. *"The Herald?* Don't you mean *The Beacon?"*

"No, sir. *The Herald.* It's our high school paper. We're working on a series of environmental stories. That's why we want to talk to you."

Now he looked confused.

"I have nothing to do with environmental issues — "

"We're doing a piece on the landfill project," I said, before he could slip back through the door. "And since you're a partner in the consortium that owns the land — "

129

"*Was* a partner," he corrected. "Sorry, kids, you've been misinformed. All I ever did was lose money on that deal, and that's not much of a story, is it? Except maybe a cautionary tale — make sure when you buy something that you're not going to have to turn around a few years later and sell it for a fraction of what you paid for it." He shook his head. "I sold my interest in the deal over a year ago."

That was a surprise. "Too bad," I said. "Especially since now whoever you sold it to is going to make a bundle." He swiveled back to face me. Now I had his attention.

"What? What do you mean?"

I put on my best baffled expression. "Haven't you heard the news?" Apparently he hadn't. "It looks like the project is going ahead."

"You must be mistaken."

"Mr. Chartoff told us."

"Bob Chartoff?"

I nodded. "He said he felt pretty foolish for not having held on to the land. He said you and Mr. Himmel were going to get rich."

"Are you sure?" Mr. Simla said.

"We only know what Mr. Chartoff told us — "

I think Mr. Simla had forgotten that the security guard was there, because when he noticed him now, a look of annoyance crossed his face. "Don't you have some rounds to make, Rudy?" he said.

Either Rudy did or he knew to back off when told to. He slunk away.

"I sold my interest to Norman Himmel," Mr. Simla said. He didn't look too happy about it.

"Gee," I said. "That's too bad."

"I bet he knew."

"Sir?" I asked.

"I bet Himmel knew this was going to happen. I sold him my interest for a fraction of what I paid to get in on it. And after all I did to make that deal happen — " He stopped abruptly. "I don't see how I can help you kids." He turned and started to punch in his security code on the keypad.

"Mr. Simla?"

The light on the keypad turned from red to green. Mr. Simla glanced back at me, but he looked distracted, as if he were thinking about the land and about the money he wasn't going to make. "I'm sorry," he said, "I have work to do." He pulled open the door.

"Mr. Simla, we think maybe Harold Shackleton is innocent," I said. "What do you think?"

Me, I think Mr. Simla was taken completely by surprise. It seemed to take him a moment to focus on me and what I was saying.

"What do I think?"

"Do you think Harold Shackleton killed his wife because she wouldn't sell the land?"

He shook his head slowly. "I don't know," he said, "but when I called Harold into my office and explained to him exactly how much money he could make if he convinced his wife to sell her land, it was like watching the tumblers of a safe clicking into place. He was planning how he was going to spend that money before I even finished making my pitch to him. I still can't understand why he couldn't make his wife see it. But obviously he couldn't."

"Were you friends with Harold Shackleton? I mean, were you ever at the Shackleton's house?" I asked.

Fred Simla looked surprised, but he said, "No."

"You're sure?"

"Look, I don't know where this is leading — "

"Where were you the morning Mrs. Shackleton was killed?" I asked. I heard Ross gasp behind me. But then, Ross looked at things differently than I did. The way I see it, you'll never know if you don't ask, and if you don't ask, you have no right to complain that you don't know. Besides, Fred Simla didn't get mad. He didn't threaten us. He didn't even call Rudy back. Instead, he smiled. Then he laughed.

"What are you, some kind of junior detective?" he said. "I was the same place I was every weekday morning at that time. I was sitting in my office. I have a dozen witnesses. Now, unless you have another bomb to drop on me . . . "

"So?" Ross said when we got back into the car.

"So, you feel like a drive to Morrisville?"

"Right now?"

"It's like eating Brussels sprouts," I said. "I know you're not enjoying this, Ross. Why don't we just get it over with?"

He sighed. Then he nodded.

Chapter 11

What is it with guys and cars? Ross's mouth fell open the moment we entered the showroom of the Morrisville car dealership. He stumbled through the immense space the way a chocoholic might move through a chocolate factory — slowly, stopping every step or two to gape at his surroundings. I'm not one hundred percent positive, but I think he was drooling. Too much shiny chrome in one place, I guess.

"Ross?"

He was standing motionless in front of a deep-amethyst ATV, staring at it as if it were everything he had ever wanted in life.

"Ross, get a grip. It's just a car!"

"*Just* a car?" Ross tore his eyes from the vehicle to look incredulously at me. "That's like calling a thoroughbred just a horse."

Okay, I could see what I was up against. I left Ross where he was, salivating all over the ATV, and approached the nearest person wearing a name tag. He smiled at me. In fact, every name tag in the place was smiling. It was like being in Disneyland. I asked where I could find Norman Himmel.

"Back office," said Phil, according to his name tag. He nodded toward a narrow corridor that led off the showroom.

I glanced back at Ross, who was still transfixed

by the car of his dreams. Then I headed down the corridor alone. The office at the end of it was, in fact, two offices. The outer office was occupied by a young woman who didn't look much older than me. She wore a name tag that said Sally. I was beginning to feel like the only person in the place whose name wasn't displayed on her chest. Sally was poring intently over a loose-leaf binder.

"Excuse me, but are you Mr. Himmel's secretary?" I asked.

Her grim expression as she looked up at me told me I had guessed wrong.

"I'm his *assistant,*" she said, "and for your information, I'm training for a position in sales. And if you think that's easy" — which I didn't. I didn't even have an opinion on the subject — "you'd better think again. I have to memorize all this stuff." She nodded at the binder. "Every vehicle has different standard features and different options, and I have to know them all by heart."

"Sounds worse than high school history," I said sympathetically. I really wanted to see Norman Himmel, but it looked like I had to get past this wannabe car salesperson first. Time to make nice.

"It's way harder than history," she said. "But you know what? You can make tons more money selling cars than you can teaching history. Plus you get incredible financing on any vehicle on the lot. I've got my eye on that black Jeep out front. Did you see it?"

I nodded, even though I didn't remember a black Jeep, and tried to look appropriately impressed.

Then I said, "Is Mr. Himmel in?"

"He's with someone." Sally inspected me closely. "You look kind of young to be buying a car."

"I want to talk to him about something else."

"Oh."

I thought she was going to ask me what, but she didn't. Instead she said, "You might as well take a load off." She nodded at a chair near a potted palm. Then she said, "Don't mind me, but I have to study." She bent over the fat binder again.

I waited. And waited.

"Excuse me," I said at last. "Are you sure Mr. Himmel is in there?"

Sally nodded. "He's in there all right." She rubbed her eyes and flipped her binder closed. "You want me to tell him you're here?"

"No, it's okay. I can wait." Then, because it didn't look like she was going to start studying again right away, I said, "Have you worked here for long?"

"Over five years," she said, which surprised me. Obviously she was older than I thought.

She closed her eyes. "I wore a brand-new navy blue linen suit to the interview, cream-colored blouse, small gold earrings — nothing flashy. Mr. Himmel wore a light gray suit, dark gray tie, white shirt, black wingtips." She opened her eyes again and smiled at me. "He hired me on the spot. Not before he made me sweat, though."

If she could remember the details of a day that long ago, she had more than enough brain power to memorize the contents of that binder.

"I guess that was a big day, huh?" I said, to be polite.

"A day like that really sticks in your mind," she said.

"Yeah," I said. "There's nothing more exciting than landing a job." Personally, I would rather have my teeth extracted one by one without the benefit of numbing than have to sit at a desk all day memorizing the features and options of anything as boring as cars.

"You have no idea how much I wanted to work here," Sally said. "It was exciting enough just to get the interview. I made sure to be right on time, just like they say you should be. In fact, I asked a friend of mine whose uncle worked here and he told me the one thing Mr. Himmel hates is not being on time, so I got here at exactly five minutes to ten, and guess what? He didn't show up until nearly forty-five minutes later. Nobody knew where he was. I thought maybe he had canceled the interview and forgotten to tell me."

"All's well that ends well," I said, and glanced at the door to Norman Himmel's office. I wished he would hurry up and save me from Sally's enthusiasm.

"I guess you could say that," she rattled on. "But at the time I was sure I wasn't going to get the job. The interview didn't go so well. Mr. Himmel didn't do much talking. It wasn't like any other job interview I'd ever had. I thought he was so quiet because he wasn't impressed with me. Guess I was wrong, huh?" I nodded because she seemed to expect me to. "I was walking on air when I left this place. Then I got home and found out there had been a murder. That's why I remember the day so well, you see."

Say what? "A murder?" Surely she didn't mean she got home and found a corpse in her house.

"A woman my mother knew. You know, that woman who was killed down in East Hastings."

"Mary Shackleton?"

She nodded.

Just then, the door to the next office opened and a man and woman came out. Neither of them looked at me, but I couldn't help staring at them as they walked past me and disappeared down the hall. I had seen the woman before, in East Hastings. I had seen her being kissed by Dave McDermott.

"Is that Mr. Himmel?" I asked Sally.

"Mr. Himmel and his wife," she said.

Mr. Himmel's wife? Why had Mr. Himmel's wife been kissing Dave McDermott?

"She looks familiar," I said.

"She comes by here all the time."

"But I don't. I'm from East Hastings, and I'm pretty sure I've seen her there."

Sally shrugged. "I wouldn't be surprised. Her brother lives there. He's the mayor."

That was interesting. I was about to ask her something else when Norman Himmel re-appeared. I stood up.

"Mr. Himmel?" I said.

He turned and peered at me, smiling the same

amiable smile I had seen on every salesperson in the showroom. I guessed he must be sizing me up, maybe thinking the same thing Sally had — that I looked a little young to be buying a car.

"Mr. Himmel, my name is Chloe Yan."

I'd never seen a smile slip so quickly off a face. If it had been made of glass, it would have shattered on the floor. He started to move past me. I trotted after him, but he turned in his office door, blocking my way into it.

"I'm going to ask you to leave," he said. "If you don't leave, I'm going to have you removed."

"I just wanted to talk to you about — "

"I know what you want to talk to me about. I'm not interested in talking to you about the landfill project or about Harold Shackleton. I have nothing to say to you. Please leave."

I had a half-dozen questions I wanted to ask him, but what would be the point? He would only refuse to answer. He would probably summon some of the name tags from the showroom. They would probably be smiling as they threw me off the property. And somehow or other, that information would get back to Levesque — I wasn't sure how, but it would. I thought about all that, then I held up my hands in surrender and said, "Okay, okay. I'm leaving."

I made my way back down the hall, going, but not going too quickly. I didn't want to look as if I were afraid of the guy. I found Ross in the showroom — still drooling over the deep-amethyst ATV — and dragged him, protesting, out of the place.

"Thanks for your help," I said, once we were back in the car.

"Did you find out anything?"

"He refused to talk to me. Someone told him about us. He clammed up as soon as I mentioned my name."

"You think maybe he has something to hide?"

I was sure he did. First, like everyone else involved in the North Mines Landfill project, he had a reason to kill Mary Shackleton — profit. Second, unlike Fred Simla and Bob Chartoff, Norman Himmel had acted like a man with a secret. And, finally, from what Sally had told me, he had deviated from his normal pattern of behavior — Mr. Punctuality had shown up forty-five minutes later than he was supposed to. I had been around Levesque long enough to know that a good investigator looks for that kind of thing. Say someone shows up at the same time in the same restaurant every Tuesday and orders the same meal. Then, one week, he shows up late. Or he doesn't show up at all. Or he orders something completely different. That sets off alarm bells — why did good old so-and-so suddenly change his pattern of behavior?

Why had good old Norman Himmel, who was a stickler for punctuality, according to Sally, kept her waiting? Why didn't anyone know where he was? Why had he been so quiet during the job interview with his new assistant? And why had he reacted so strongly to my appearance — none of his partners in the consortium had been overly bothered by me or my questions. And wasn't it interesting that

Dave McDermott, the investigating officer in the Mary Shackleton murder, was Norman Himmel's brother-in-law? What if McDermott had pinned the crime on Harold Shackleton in order to protect his brother-in-law? Was that possible?

"Interesting theory," Ross said, after I had laid it all out for him. "Except that Dave McDermott's sister didn't get married until two years ago — my mother went to the wedding. For all I know, McDermott's sister didn't even know Norman Himmel when Mary Shackleton was killed."

Oh.

"But it's still possible that Himmel did it," I said. And it was. He had deviated from his normal routine.

"How do you plan to try to prove that?" Ross said.

Good question.

We drove back to East Hastings in silence. Ross dropped me on Centre Street.

"Sorry I can't drive you home," he said, "but I have to pick up my little sister at Brownies. I can just about make it."

"No problem," I told him. "And Ross? Thanks for your help."

He shrugged. "I'm not sure it's getting you anywhere," he said, "but you're welcome."

I stood on the sidewalk shivering while I watched Ross's running lights disappear around a corner. Then I shoved my hands deep into my pockets and headed over to the police station. The place was deserted except for Officer Steve Denby.

"Levesque's not here," he said.

I shrugged. "It's no big deal," I said. "I was just passing by. I thought we could go home together." Then, because I was brought up right, which means that the rudiments of good manners had been pounded into my head, I said, "So, how are you doing, Steve?"

"Okay, I guess." He couldn't have sounded less enthusiastic if he'd been lobotomized. I peered at him for a moment while those good manners of mine battled with sheer curiosity. There could have been a thousand and one reasons why Steve Denby seemed blue. It could have been girlfriend trouble. Or maybe he had been chewed out by Levesque. Or maybe sweet-faced Steve had finally taken a good look around him and had decided, as I did at least once a week, that small-town life has all the excitement of, say, a bowl of oatmeal. None of which was any of my business unless he signaled that he wanted to share his innermost thoughts with me, which he didn't.

"Okay, well, I guess I'll see you then," I said. I waited a moment before heading for the door, just in case he decided he wanted to tell me something. He didn't.

I got home just as Mom was stacking the supper dishes in the dishwasher. The house seemed un- usually quiet — well, except for Shendor jumping up on me and barking.

"Where is everyone?" I asked. Then, "Down, girl." I might as well have recited a geometry theorem to her, for all the attention she paid.

"Where have *you* been?" my mother said. It wasn't

141

the answer I was looking for.

"Ross and I were working on a story."

My mother wrapped her hands around Shendor's muzzle and stared her straight in the eyes. Amazingly, the dog settled. I began to wonder if there had been a dog somewhere in Mom's past. Then Mom turned her attention back to me.

"You remember that handy device called the telephone?"

Uh-oh. When my mother started to get sarcastic, it was definitely time to dive for cover. I moved over to the dishwasher and started to help her — you could call it a diversionary tactic.

"Where's Phoebe?" I asked.

"Debating."

Phoebe was on the junior debating team.

"Where's Lev . . . Where's Louis?" Mom wished with all her heart that I would call him Dad. He didn't insist on it, though. Call me Louis, he said. Most of the time I managed to skirt the whole issue by not calling him anything at all. But I always thought of him as if I were reading about him in a newspaper. I always thought of him as Levesque.

"He went down to Toronto for a couple of days."

"Oh?" He hadn't mentioned any trip to Toronto. "How come?"

My mother turned on the water in the sink and squirted some dish detergent into a casserole dish.

"Have you eaten yet?" she asked me. "Are you hungry?"

I hadn't, and I was, and I said so. After she set the casserole dish to soak in the sink, she started to fish leftovers out of the fridge. She still hadn't answered my question.

"So how come he went down to Toronto?" I asked again.

My mother set a big slice of lasagna on a plate, put the plate into the microwave, and pushed a bunch of buttons. "It's a business trip," she said. She didn't sound very happy about it. "He'll be back in a couple of days." She went back to the fridge and pulled out a container of coleslaw and a jug of milk. She poured some milk and set it on the table. When the microwave beeped, she took out the plate and spooned some coleslaw on it. Then she set that on the table and motioned for me to sit down, which I did, while she scurried around again putting everything away.

"Mom," I said, "is everything okay?"

"What do you mean?" she said. I would have had to have been blind not to see her lip tremble.

"Are you and Lev . . . Are you two having problems?" I asked. "Is that why he went to Toronto?"

My mother seemed completely surprised by the question. "No," she said, and never had one word carried so much emotion. "Why would you ask a thing like that?"

"You seem upset about something."

She managed a wan smile. "Just a bad day," she said. "I did a double shift at work. My feet are sore. Everyone seemed to have a problem. And I was worried when you didn't come home for supper and didn't call."

I reached out and squeezed her hand. "Well, I'm

home now and I'm starving," I said. I dug into her lasagna with gusto. I wished Levesque wasn't out of town. I could have told him about Norman Himmel and got him — well, tried to get him — to look into Himmel's whereabouts that morning. Now it looked like I was going to have to wait a few days. Either that or come up with some way to check things out myself.

Chapter 12

I was thinking about Jonah on my way to school on Monday. I had thought about him all weekend. Agonized about him, in fact. Should I tell him my suspicions about Norman Himmel, or should I wait and see if someone could alibi Himmel? I couldn't make up my mind. On the one hand, I didn't want to get Jonah's hopes up only to have to dash them. *Hey, what do you know. I made a mistake, it wasn't Norman Himmel after all.* On the other hand, I kept thinking that if I were in Jonah's shoes and if I knew someone had found out something — anything — about what had really happened to my mother, I'd want that person to share that information with me, no matter what. Back to the first hand, Jonah knew that Ross and I were going to see Fred Simla and Norman Himmel, but he hadn't made any attempt to find out what we had learned.

I had almost decided to tell Jonah what I knew when I spotted him up ahead. It wasn't exactly needle-in-a-haystack spotting, though. As far as I could tell, everyone on Centre Street had spotted — and was staring at — Jonah and the person he was yelling at. That person was Dave McDermott.

"You had no right," Jonah was saying. His face was red, but not, in my opinion, from the cold. It was the red of rage. "You had no right at all."

In contrast to Jonah, Dave McDermott was perfectly calm.

"I don't think you know what you're talking about," he said. "Now if you'll excuse me — "

Jonah blocked his path.

"I want you to call him back," he said. "I want you to tell him that everything is fine, that there's nothing to worry about."

Dave McDermott looked directly into Jonah's eyes for a few moments. Then he shrugged and glanced at the people who had stopped to watch. He shook his head slowly.

"If I really believed there was nothing to worry about, I wouldn't have said anything in the first place," Dave McDermott said. "I know you don't think too highly of me, Jonah. But I know how important you and your brother are to your father. And I've known your dad for a long time. I know he worries about the two of you and your aunt."

I saw Jonah's whole body tense. I saw his right hand curl into a fist and I saw that fist start to swing back. I rushed over to him and grabbed his hand.

"Hey, Jonah, I've been looking for you."

He tried to shake free of me, but I held on tight. Dave McDermott nodded, as if he were glad to see me.

"You need to calm down, Jonah," he said. "You need to concentrate on your schoolwork and on staying out of trouble. That's what your dad wants. You know it is."

Jonah's fist didn't unclench. If anything, it got

tighter and harder. I didn't know why he was so mad, but I did know that the faster I could get him away from McDermott, the better.

"Come on," I said. I pulled on his arm. It was like trying to drag a boulder through a swamp. "Come *on,*" I said again, and yanked even harder at him. He started to move with me, but only reluctantly. "The one thing you don't need more of," I said, "is trouble."

"I hate him," he said.

"Really? Gee, how come I didn't pick up on that? I guess the old radar isn't working as well as it should be." I kept a firm grip on his arm, and dragged him farther and farther from Dave McDermott. "What is it with you, anyway? Are you *trying* to get yourself arrested?"

Talk about putting a match to the fuse on a stick of dynamite. Jonah's temper exploded. He shook free of my grip.

"What do you know about it?" he said. "You have no idea what he did!"

He was wrong. I had an idea — McDermott had talked to Jonah's father and that had sparked Jonah's anger. But I didn't know the whole story. Maybe now was a good time to hear it.

"I'm sorry," I said.

I've discovered that those are two of the most magical words in the world. I think that's because most people don't hear them often enough. Nobody likes to admit that they're wrong or that they've done something they shouldn't have, which pretty much means that nobody likes to apologize. Which, in turn, means that people who feel they've been

147

wronged rarely hear the two words that I had just spoken to Jonah. Personally, I don't mind saying them. No one's perfect, right? Isn't that what parents always tell you? And teachers. If no one's perfect, then it stands to reason that everyone makes mistakes. And if making mistakes is as natural as breathing, then it also stands to reason that saying, oops, I messed up, sorry about that, should be as common as, well, as messing up in the first place. But it isn't, which gives an edge to people like me who know how much people love to be told, "You're right, I was wrong."

"I wasn't thinking," I said to Jonah. "I just wanted to make sure you didn't take a swing at McDermott and end up getting charged with assault. What's going on?"

"I hate him," Jonah said again.

"So you said."

I waited. He tramped along beside me without saying a word, down the street, then up the hill toward school, and still I waited. Don't be in a rush to fill the silence, Levesque had told me once. Silence makes people uncomfortable. If you bide your time and hold your tongue, the other person will eventually feel compelled to speak and maybe, just maybe, you'll learn something.

"My dad phoned last night," Jonah said at last.

I waited a little longer.

"McDermott called my dad to tell him how hard things have been for Aunt Linda. He told Dad what I've been doing. He told him that I was getting into trouble. He told him about Jay, too, about

148

the problems Jay's started having again."

"How did McDermott know about that?"

"He heard that Jay had run off. I think a lot of people heard about that. Aunt Linda got all hysterical when we couldn't find him for those few hours. Maybe the rest he found out from some of the other waitresses at Stella's," he said. "Or maybe one of Jay's teachers said something. He's been having trouble at school. His teacher told Aunt Linda that Jay has been fighting with other kids ever since — " His voice broke off. He turned away from me and wiped his nose. At least, I think it was his nose. I burrowed in my pocket for a tissue and handed it to him. "It's all my fault," he said.

"It's your fault Jay's been having trouble at school?"

"I made a big deal marching up and down in front of the municipal building. I got the press involved. Kids who didn't know anything about my dad, kids like Jay who were just babies when it happened, heard all about it because of what I did. They started giving Jay a hard time. You don't know how he is. He seems really quiet, and most of the time he is. He keeps everything inside until the pressure builds up, and then all of a sudden he explodes. Aunt Linda tries. She really does. But she's having a hard time handling everything. And so what does good old Dave McDermott do? He tells my dad what's been happening. He pretends to be all concerned about me and Jay — he doesn't care about us at all. But he tells my dad he is. He tells him everything that's been going on, and the next thing I know my dad's calling me, which he doesn't get to do very often. McDermott must have helped him. He sounded so upset. He told me not to worry about him. He told me to worry about myself instead, and to look after Jay and Aunt Linda. He told me he wasn't worth worrying about. What's that supposed to mean?" He peered at me. "Why wouldn't he be worth worrying about?"

It was a funny thing for Harold Shackleton to have said.

"I tried to tell him everything was okay," Jonah said, "but he had to get off the phone. I could tell he was still upset when he hung up." His voice sounded funny, all quivery. "He told me I never should have sent those e-mails, I never should have made those signs. He told me it wasn't worth it." That seemed to bother him a lot. "Why would he say that?"

"He's just worried about you," I said. "He doesn't want anything to happen to you or Jay on account of him." And Dave McDermott was obviously worried about his upcoming election plans.

"It's already happened," he said. "It happened when he got sent to prison." I saw his fists clench at his side again. If there had been a tree or a lamppost, I was pretty sure Jonah would have slammed one of his fists into it. "I never told my dad, you know. With all the things he has to deal with, I never told him what McDermott did after."

I frowned. "What do you mean?"

"Dave McDermott was one of my dad's best friends," Jonah said.

I stared at him and prayed that I would never be blessed with a friend like that.

"At least, I *thought* he was Dad's friend," Jonah said. His voice was bitter. "And I'm pretty sure that's what Dad thought, too. He and McDermott curled on the same team. Dad was skip. Dave was second. He used to come over to the house all the time. Used to stay for dinner. I thought he was my friend too. Was I ever stupid!" His eyes glistened. He wasn't exactly crying, but he looked close to it. "He used to toss a baseball around with me. Took me fishing a couple of times too. He acted like a friend. A grown-up friend, but a friend just the same, you know?" I didn't really know, but I nodded anyway. "Then, after Mom died, everything changed. He arrested Dad and, sure, you could say he was just doing his job. But after Dad went to prison, McDermott stopped coming around. No more baseball. No more fishing. It was like we were this big criminal family and he didn't want to be seen with us anymore. And now he's gone and made things worse. My dad's upset. Aunt Linda's upset. I don't know how he can get Aunt Linda all churned up, especially when — " He broke off suddenly and pulled himself up straight. He drew in a deep breath and wiped at his eyes with the palms of his hands.

"Especially when what?" I asked.

"Nothing," he said. Now his eyes were dry. His voice was under control. He had that determined look in his eyes again, the one that made me think trouble was just around the corner. "Nothing. I hate him. And the less I think about him, the better."

We were right across the street from school now. The bell would ring any minute, but Jonah turned away.

"Where are you going?" I asked.

"I have stuff to do."

"But Jonah — "

But nothing. He was striding away from me. Half of me wanted to chase after him, but I didn't think it would do any good. Instead, I headed for school and the newspaper office. I had to find Ross.

* * *

"Hey, guess what?" Ross said, before I could even make my request. "I was right. I asked my mom and she confirmed that McDermott's sister only married Norman Himmel two years ago."

I sagged a little at the news, but it still didn't rule Himmel out as a suspect as far as I was concerned.

"But," Ross said after a short pause, "she *was* going out with him long before that. And guess how she met Himmel?"

I waited.

"Himmel and McDermott went to high school together."

"Here in East Hastings?"

Ross shook his head. "In North Bay. They're both from North Bay."

Perfect. I asked Ross what I had come to ask him

"Not today," he said.

"But it's important," I said.

"I know."

"Well, then?"

"Look, Chloe, I can't get the car today. It could be a life-and-death situation, and I still wouldn't be able to drive you back to Morrisville today. Sorry."

"What about tomorrow?"

He thought it over. "I could do it tomorrow."

"Promise?"

"Promise," he said.

* * *

"This is crazy," Ross said at seven-thirty the next morning.

I pried the lid off his cup of coffee and set it into the cup holder where he would be able to reach it.

"The early bird catches the worm," I said.

Ross shot me a glance that could have withered grapes into raisins in a flash.

"First of all," he said, "we're looking for people, not worms. Specifically, people who will be able to tell us something about Norman Himmel's whereabouts on a particular day five years ago. What makes you think anyone is going to remember a thing like that? Second, no matter how you cut it, we're going to get into trouble for cutting class. Even if I break all the speed limits — which I have no intention of doing, so don't even ask me — we can't get to Morrisville, ask around, and get back to East Hastings before at least third period." He shook his head. "I don't know why I let you talk me into this."

It hadn't actually taken much talking. In fact, not that he would admit it, but our little excursion had been Ross's idea. Well, sort of. I guess techni-

153

cally it was Sally the wannabe salesperson who had planted the seed in my mind. But it was Ross who made it germinate.

"You always hear that people can remember exactly what they were doing when they found out that John F. Kennedy had been assassinated," he had said on the way back from our first visit to Norman Himmel, after I had told him everything that had happened. "Or when they heard that Princess Diana had been killed in that car accident."

"Most people in North America were asleep when that news hit the air waves," I'd pointed out.

Ross had waved aside that point. "When Jonah was on the news the other day, my mom told me she has a perfect memory of the day Mary Shackleton was killed. She says she was going for her coffee break and she decided to run across the street to Stella's to get a cinnamon bun. She says it was funny because she almost never ate cinnamon buns because they were fattening and she was on a diet. But that morning she couldn't stand it anymore, she wanted something sweet and sticky. So she ran over to Stella's and when she got there one of the waitresses was crying. They had just heard the news about Mary Shackleton."

"Gee, that's interesting, Ross," I'd said. Interesting, I had thought at the time, but hardly relevant.

He had given me that you-city-people-never-understand-anything look of his. "People don't get murdered around here," he said with excruciating patience. "So when a murder does happen, it tends to stick in people's minds."

It had certainly stuck in Sally's mind.

I hadn't given that much thought at the time. In fact, Ross's words hadn't floated to the surface of my consciousness again until I started thinking about Norman Himmel.

"Somebody will remember something," I said to him now. "Your mother remembered what she was doing that day. So did Sally."

"Yeah, but — "

"So I bet if we were to ask, people would be able to tell us what they were doing when they heard that Mary Shackleton was murdered. I bet they'd be able to remember a lot about that morning."

He glanced at me. "Like whether they remember seeing Norman Himmel?"

I nodded.

"Where are we going to start when we get there?" he said.

"With Mrs. Himmel."

"What if she didn't see him that morning? After all, they were just going out. They weren't even engaged or anything."

"What if she did see him? Or what if he said something to her about that morning?" It was worth a try.

* * *

Finding Mrs. Himmel turned out to be not as easy as I had hoped, mainly because she wasn't home.

"The best-laid plans," I said with a shrug as we turned away from the Himmels' front door.

"Hey, you kids," someone yelled at us. A man with a small dog on a leash scowled at us from the foot of the driveway. "What are you kids up to?"

"Nosy old — " Ross muttered under his breath.

I pasted on my best smile and walked down the driveway toward the man. You never know, right?

"We're looking for Mrs. Himmel," I said.

"Well, you won't find her there."

"No kidding," Ross grumbled. I elbowed him in the ribs.

"*Bichon frise,* right?" I asked, and bent down to let his little dog sniff my hand. "What's her name?"

"Cecily."

I scratched the dog behind the ear. "Hi, Cecily," I cooed. Then I looked back up at the man. "I have a dog, too. A golden retriever." His expression softened. Dog people like other dog people. "Do you know where we could find Mrs. Himmel?"

"You could try her at work."

I continued to smile expectantly at him while I scratched little Cecily's ear.

"The veterinary clinic up near the highway," the man said.

I thanked him and we were on our way.

We found the clinic without too much trouble and even though it wasn't quite nine o'clock, someone was in it. I asked the woman at the desk if Mrs. Himmel was in the building. The woman — who was wearing a name tag that said *Lois* — was getting the impression that wearing name tags was a municipal bylaw in Morrisville — shook her head.

"There's no Mrs. Himmel here," she said.

"We were told we would find her here."

"I'm afraid there's no one here by that name," she said. Then she grinned. "There is a Dr. McDermott, though," she said.

Dave McDermott's sister had kept her own name when she married. And she didn't just *work* at the veterinary clinic. She was the vet. I slapped my forehead for Lois's benefit.

"My dad suggested we talk to her," I said. "My dad is a business associate of Mr. Himmel's. He's also a bit of a Neanderthal. He always refers to her as Mrs. Himmel."

"She hates that," Lois said.

I tried to look apologetic on my so-called dad's behalf. "Is Dr. McDermott in?"

"She's out on a call."

"Do you know when she'll be back?"

She shook her head. "She went out to Millrock Stables. She could be out for most of the morning."

"That figures," Ross muttered.

"Do you want to leave her a message?" Lois said.

I glanced at Ross, who shook his head.

"Actually," I said, "maybe you could help us." Lois smiled obligingly. "We wanted to talk to Dr. McDermott because we're doing a scientific experiment for school, and my dad suggested that since she's a vet and everything . . . " I let that thought hang. "But I bet you know a lot about scientific method, too," I said. "So I bet you can help us."

Lois looked a little doubtful now, but she kept on smiling.

"The experiment is about memory recall," I said. "We're trying to show how certain key events can trigger a cascade of memories. It's a kind of where-were-you-when experiment." Lois was nodding along with me, and I had to admit, our little non-project sounded interesting. "Would you be willing to help us out?" I said. "Would you mind being one of our subjects?"

"Well, sure, I guess," Lois said.

"We're asking people to think back five years," I said. I glanced over at Ross, who was staring somewhat stupidly at me. *Sorry, Ross.* "Aren't you going to take notes?" I asked him. He continued to stare stupidly at me — *Sorry again, Ross* — then fumbled in his jacket pocket for a notebook. "Were you working here five years ago, Lois? May I call you Lois?"

Lois patted her name tag. "That's my name."

I smiled at her. "I'm Chloe, and this is Ross. Okay, so here's the trigger. We're using an event that's rare around here — murder."

"Oh, my," said Lois.

"Five years ago, a woman was murdered in East Hastings — "

"Mary Shackleton, right?" Lois called out, as if she had her thumb on a *Jeopardy* buzzer. She seemed quite proud of herself.

"Right," I said. "Wow, you really have a good memory. Here's the big question — do you remember exactly what you were doing when you heard that the first murder in this area in nearly fifty years had just been committed?"

Lois didn't even bat an eye. "Why, sure," she said. " was right here. In fact, I was the one who answere

158

the phone when Mr. Himmel called with the news."

"Dr. McDermott's husband told you that Mary Shackleton had been murdered?" I said.

"No, he told Dr. McDermott and Dr. McDermott told me. Except Dr. McDermott wasn't Mr. Himmel's wife then. She had just started seeing him."

I nodded and glanced at Ross. He had caught the spirit of the thing now and was writing everything down.

"Okay. So you heard that Mary Shackleton had been murdered just after Mr. Himmel called. Is that right?"

Lois nodded.

"Now this is a hard one, Lois. Probably the hardest question there is. Do you remember what time it was when Mr. Himmel called with that news?"

Lois puffed up proudly. "It was exactly twelve-thirty."

I don't know what I had expected, but I sure hadn't expected something so definite.

"How do you know?"

Her eyes misted up. "Bunny Rosenberg had just died."

"Bunny Rosenberg?"

"Zachary Rosenberg's rabbit. He had a tumor. Dr. McDermott tried to save him, but he died and Dr. McDermott had just asked me to note the time so she could write it down in her file. Then the phone rang and I answered it. It was Mr. Himmel." She paused a moment and thought. "He sounded upset. He wanted to talk to Dr. McDermott right away, but I had to put him on hold for a few minutes.

Zachary Rosenberg was here and Dr. McDermott was giving him the bad news. In fact," she said, her eyes lighting up as more and more details came back to her — we had lucked onto something big with this memory trigger stuff — "I had to check back with Mr. Himmel three or four times, because Zachary wasn't taking the news all that well. And every time I told Mr. Himmel, I'm sorry, but it's going to be another couple of minutes, he got more and more excited. He sounded so upset that I thought maybe the axe had finally fallen on the Breakfast Club."

"The Breakfast Club?"

"Mr. Himmel volunteered at the Breakfast Club. He's been doing it for years. It's a hot breakfast program for kids who come to school hungry. Mr. Himmel was there two mornings a week — Tuesday and Thursday — from seven until eight-thirty, cooking breakfast. It was on a Thursday that Mary Shackleton was murdered."

My hope deflated. If Norman Himmel was serving breakfast in Morrisville until eight-thirty in the morning, he couldn't have been in East Hastings much before nine-thirty. Linda Shackleton had found her sister-in-law at the bottom of the basement stairs at five minutes after eleven. The pathologist had said that by then, Mary Shackleton had been dead for a couple of hours. Which meant that if Norman Himmel hadn't been in East Hastings until nine-thirty, he couldn't have done it. But if Norman Himmel had served breakfast here in Morrisville until eight-thirty and he had never left town, why had he shown up forty-five minutes late for his ten o'clock interview with Sally?

"Well, how did I do?" Lois said.

I forced myself to smile.

"You did great." I nodded at Ross and he closed his notebook. Then I said to Lois, "This Breakfast Club sounds like a good idea. We don't have one in East Hastings. You don't happen to know who runs the program here, do you? We'd love to find out more about it, wouldn't we, Ross?"

Ross nodded on cue.

Lois gave us the name of the teacher at the local elementary school who coordinated the program. We thanked her and headed off to find the school.

* * *

We found Ms. Henderson marking arithmetic tests in her classroom during morning recess. She liked the idea of our experiment so much that she made a note of it in her lesson planner. "I don't think your teacher would mind if I borrowed a good idea, do you?" she said.

"Not at all." I waited until she had finished her note. Then, "So, what do you remember about that day Mary Shackleton was murdered?"

She thought a moment. "It's quite odd, really," she said, "because just that morning — this was *before* I heard the news — I remember thinking to myself that the day couldn't possibly get any worse."

"Oh?"

"That morning I had come to school early, as usual. It was a Thursday. The person who volun-

161

teered at the Breakfast Club with me was supposed to have been here to help me, but when I arrived, he wasn't here."

"Was that Norman Himmel?" I asked.

She gave me an odd look, but nodded.

"I found out later that something had come up at work, some kind of emergency. But at the time, all I knew was that I had thirty breakfasts to prepare and no help. I just about had the oatmeal under control when I got a call from the county department of social services. At seven-fifteen!" She shook her head again. Obviously the county department of social services wasn't in the habit of calling so early. "They were holding a special meeting for ten o'clock that morning on the future funding of the breakfast program and they wanted me there. I didn't want to go without Norman. He was the one who helped get the funding for the program in the first place. He really cares about this community. So between the oatmeal and the toast and peanut butter, I called his office, but he wasn't there."

She had sort of an astonished look on her face. "Gosh," she said, "I haven't thought about any of this for years. This is really quite amazing."

I smiled. Ross straightened up a little and stopped looking embarrassed.

"So you called Mr. Himmel and . . . ?"

"He wasn't there. I called a couple of times that morning, but I couldn't get hold of him. Well, I was dreading going to that meeting alone, I can tell you. But in the end, I had no choice. I went and i turned out that the news was good, not bad. The funding for the program was renewed. In fact, we got more money, which is why they called us so early. They wanted to make sure someone from the program showed up for the big announcement. The meeting took about an hour. I came back to the school. We celebrated. And then we heard that there had been a murder in East Hastings and that it was Mary Shackleton."

"Did you know her?" I asked.

"No, but I knew of her. I think just about everyone in the area did." She shook her head again, and then offered me a little smile. "That's quite an experiment. It sounds to me as if you're not going to have too much trouble proving your theory."

I glanced at Ross and saw the same expression on his face that I know I was wearing on mine — a not-too-subtle look of hope. Norman Himmel hadn't shown up to prepare breakfast that morning. He had said he was in his office, but Ms. Henderson hadn't been able to get hold of him. He had shown up forty-five minutes late for his interview with Sally and no one knew where he was before that. All of which meant that he *could* have driven down to East Hastings, pushed Mary Shackleton down the stairs, then driven back here. It was possible.

* * *

Levesque wasn't home for supper that night. When I asked Mom where he was, all she said was, "Down in Toronto," which I already knew.

"What's he doing there?" I said.

"I've already told you. It's a business trip," she said, which would have been fine if I'd asked her to describe the nature of his trip, rather than the purpose of it. But I hadn't.

"What kind of business?"

Even Phoebe's interest was piqued by Mom's evasiveness.

Mom did not look happy. "For heaven's sake, Chloe, what is this? Twenty questions?"

That's right, Mom. That's exactly what this is, which means I have seventeen questions to go.

"Is he up to something he shouldn't be up to?" I said. "Is that why you don't want to talk about it?" Fifteen to go.

"Who said I didn't want to talk about it?" I think this was Mom's attempt to fight fire with fire — or, in this case, question with question.

"What do you mean, up to something?" Phoebe asked.

"Maybe he has a girlfriend in Toronto," I said. Phoebe looked properly shocked by this. "Maybe that's why Steve looked so upset when I asked him about it."

Phoebe turned to Mom. "Is it true?"

"Of course it isn't," Mom said. I sensed from the sharpness in her voice that I had pushed this about as far as I could.

"What's going on, Mom?" I asked. "Where's Levesque?"

My mother fixed me with a solemn look. "He is in Toronto on business." And that was all she said.

Chapter 13

Ross had been right about getting into trouble for missing classes, but he had been wrong about how many we would miss. We got back in time for fifth period, not third. And from what I could tell, Jonah hadn't been at school at all. Lately he seemed to be absent more than he was present. I still hadn't told him what I had found out, mostly because I didn't want to tell him what I suspected until I could prove it. I didn't want to get his hopes up only to have to send them crashing again. And there wasn't much more I could do in the way of proving it until I had a talk with Levesque. But as I was stacking the dishwasher that night, I wondered if I shouldn't tell Jonah anyway. I could make him promise to keep quiet about it until we knew everything there was to know. I could make him promise not to do something stupid. I had just about decided to go over to his aunt's house and fill him in when the phone rang.

Mom picked it up. I didn't pay any attention until I heard her say, "No, it's fine. Try to stay calm." Stay calm? Who was she talking to? What was going on? "We'll be right over," she said. "And you shouldn't drive if you're upset. Of course Chloe will stay with Jay. I'll take you to the hospital."

"Jay Shackleton?" I said when my mother hung up the phone.

She nodded. "Get your coat." Then, "Phoebe!"

"Yeah?" Phoebe called down the stairs.

"Chloe and I are going out for a while. I'll call you."

We were in the car and backing down the driveway before my mother filled me in.

"Jonah was in some kind of fight. He's in the hospital and Linda doesn't want to take Jay to the hospital with her."

"Why did she call you?" I asked. I didn't think Mom knew Linda Shackleton, except maybe casually, the way a lot of people in small towns seem to.

"Actually, she was calling you," Mom said. "She doesn't want to take Jay with her because she isn't sure how badly hurt Jonah is. And Jay refuses to stay with anyone but you." She gave me a long look. "Apparently you've made quite an impression on him."

Linda Shackleton managed a smile when she opened the door and ushered us in, but she looked as if she were fighting back tears.

"Jay!" she called. Her voice trembled. "Chloe is here."

Jay appeared in the doorway behind her. That is, a tiny patch of his hair and one of his eyes appeared. I smiled at him.

"Hi, Jay, how's it going?" I said.

The patch of hair and the lone eye vanished. Linda Shackleton sniffled. My mother laid a hand on her arm.

"Come on," she said quietly. "Chloe will look after everything here." She said it as if she had no

166

doubts about my babysitting ability. I wished I could have been even half as confident as she was.

After the door clicked shut behind Mom and Jonah's aunt, the house seemed strangely silent. I pulled off my coat and hung it in the hall closet. Then I headed for the living room to look for Jay. He wasn't there.

"Jay?"

No answer.

"Hey, Jay, would you like me to read you a story?" Then I remembered the chapter books I had seen him reading so proudly in the library while I tutored Jonah. "Or do you want to read a story to me?"

No answer.

I looked in the dining room. No Jay. Kitchen. No Jay. Laundry room. Still no Jay. Please, please, please don't let it turn out that he ran away the minute his aunt left the house. Don't let it turn out that I'm the world's worst babysitter. Then, from upstairs, I heard a crash.

I hurried toward the source of the sound and found Jay in what I assumed was his aunt's bedroom. A silver picture frame, its glass shattered, lay at his feet. Jay didn't even look around at me. He stood his ground and continued what he had been doing — ripping something, a photograph, into tiny pieces and scattering the pieces like confetti over the broken glass. The pieces of paper were so small that I couldn't make out what the picture had been — I know, because I checked later. At the time, though, all I saw was a zoned-out Jay, ripping and ripping while big blobs of blood dripped onto the mess he was making.

"Hey, Jay," I said as calmly as I could, "what are you doing?" Please, please, don't let that cut on his hand be as deep as it looks.

He didn't look at me. He didn't even seem to hear me.

I crept closer to him and touched him lightly on the shoulder. Only after he had finished shredding the photograph did he look up at me.

"We should wash that cut," I said softly, "and then we should put a bandage on it."

He frowned, as if he were struggling to decipher my words. Then he looked down at his hand. I guess he hadn't noticed that he was bleeding until I pointed it out. Once he realized it, he reacted the way a lot of little kids do. His eyes grew enormous at the sight of his own blood, and he started to cry.

"Hey, hey," I said, doing my best to sound comforting. I took his good hand in mine. "Hey, it's okay. Come on, let's go and clean that up."

I led him into the bathroom and lifted him onto the counter beside the sink. When I scooped him up, I was surprised to find he had all the weight of the little boy equivalent of a sparrow. Then I washed his wound. To my relief, it wasn't nearly as deep as I had feared. A Sesame Street Band-Aid was all the first aid he needed. Then I led him into his bedroom, a cheery yellow room plastered with hockey posters, and sat him on his bed.

"Now, how about a story?" I said.

"Where's Jonah?"

"He should be home soon," I said. Mom had said Linda Shackleton didn't know how badly he was hurt. I hoped it wasn't too serious. "I don't know about you," I said, "but I always find a good book helps pass the time. Do you want me to read to you?"

He didn't nod, but he didn't shake his head, either, so I pulled a book from the shelf beside his bed — a book about hockey superstars.

"How about this one?" I asked as I sank down onto the edge of his bed. At least, I thought it was his bed until I felt something lumpy and hard and sort of sharp under me. I jumped up again. "What the — ?" I looked down and laughed. I had sat on his teddy bear. But what had bit so sharply into me? The teddy's eyes were embroidered, not made of buttons. His nose was a soft patch of felt — nothing sharp or hard there. Then I squeezed the bear. Aha! There was something inside. Something that, judging from its effect on my posterior, could be harmful to a small boy. I squeezed the teddy again, trying to figure out what was hiding in there.

"Give me!" Jay demanded.

"But there's something inside," I said.

Jay snatched the bear out of my hands and crushed it to his small body.

"That's mine!" he said.

I could have argued with him. If he had been Phoebe, I would have yanked it away from him. But he wasn't Phoebe. He was, from everything I had heard, a troubled little boy.

"Sorry," I said. I sat down on the bed again. "So,

why don't we find out everything there is to know about Wayne Gretzky?"

I read to him about Gretzky's father flooding the backyard to make a skating rink so that Wayne could practice. Then we read about Gretzky joining the Edmonton Oilers. Then the story of how he got traded to Los Angeles, and still Jay wasn't sleepy. Every time a car passed the house, his ears pricked up and I could tell he was holding his breath, waiting to hear if a car door would open and close in the driveway. He wasn't going to sleep until he found out how his brother was.

"Come on," I said, grabbing a blanket from his bed. "Let's go watch TV."

He was curled up and covered up at one end of the couch, struggling to keep his eyes open for the late news, when he finally heard the sound he had been waiting for. And, I admit it, I found myself holding my breath this time, too. I counted the car doors closing — one . . . two . . . three. Jonah must be with them. If he was, then he couldn't be too badly hurt. Still, it seemed to take forever before a key turned in the front door. Jay leaped off the sofa.

"Jonah," he shouted as he ran out of the living room.

I got up and followed him. I was shocked at what I saw.

One of Jonah's eyes was black and blue and pretty much swollen shut. His lip had been cut; a scab had formed on it. One hand was tightly bandaged — a sprained wrist, my mother told me later. His

T-shirt was ripped. The knuckles of his unbandaged hand were cut and bruised and swollen.

Jay threw himself at Jonah. Jonah winced on impact, but said nothing. He slipped his unbandaged hand over Jay's shoulder and together they headed up the stairs.

"Is he all right?" I asked.

Linda nodded. Her eyes were red. She had been crying.

"Come on, Chloe," my mother said quietly. "We'd better get home and let everyone get some sleep."

I nodded and fetched my coat. As I slipped it on, I remembered the broken picture frame.

"Jay knocked over a picture frame on your dresser," I told Linda. "I guess he was pretty upset, because he ripped up the photo that was in it. I hope it was nothing important."

It must not have been, because she just shrugged and thanked me for coming over.

"What happened?" I asked my mother on the way home.

"He said some boys were taunting him," she said. "He lost his temper."

"But he's okay?"

She sighed. "He's a very unhappy young man," she said. "I think his aunt is worried, and I can't say that I blame her. I'd be worried, too, if I were in her shoes."

* * *

The last thing I wanted to do was go to school the next day. I didn't pay much attention in any of my classes. At lunch and after school I headed for the pay phone on the corner to call Jonah. No one answered. I stopped by Stella's on the way home, but Linda wasn't there. No one could tell me where she was. I wondered if she had taken Jonah to a doctor's appointment. I also wondered if he was okay.

Levesque came home just as Mom was starting to make supper. They did the kiss-on-the-cheek and huggy thing, him still in his jacket and boots, her with a wooden spoon in one hand and a pot holder in the other. Something was bubbling in a pot on the stove behind them, threatening to boil over. Oops, better make that actually boiling over. When my mother heard the hiss as whatever was in the pot spilled over onto the gas burner, she scurried back to her cooking. I followed Levesque into the front hall. I wanted to talk to him about Norman Himmel.

"So, what have you been up to?" I asked as I watched him hang up his jacket.

"This and that," he said, which really surprised me. The Louis Levesque I had come to know always either answered me directly or told me flat out why he wasn't going to. He was never evasive — until now.

"Let me rephrase," I said. "What were you doing down in Toronto?"

"Nothing you need to be concerned about."

Sure, Mr. Policeman. Nothing at all. Which is why you blinked like that and didn't look me straight in the eye. Correct me if I'm wrong, but aren't blinking and avoidance of eye contact tip-offs to any interrogator worth her salt that her suspect is lying?

"I appreciate your frankness," I said. I shoved by him, grabbed my coat from the closet and went outside. It was barely five o'clock yet, but the sun was pretty much down. I circled around to the back of the house and trudged down the slope of our backyard, heading toward the trees and the scrub that lay just beyond our property line and stretched . . . well, I wasn't actually sure how far it stretched. There was a rough little path that led through the woods, but I had never followed it and — call me a pathetic little city girl — but I wasn't about to follow it now, not with the sun fast disappearing, not with it being bush and, therefore, habitat for who knew what sort of wildlife. Instead I just stood there fuming.

It was ten minutes before I felt his presence behind me.

"Sorry," he said.

I didn't turn. Why should I? Not deigning to notice him didn't make him go away, however. He circled around me and stood, hands buried deep in the pockets of his sheepskin jacket, completely blocking my view.

"It sure is easy on the eyes up here, isn't it?" he said. "Trees are a lot nicer to look at than concrete, don't you think?"

"Oh, boy," I said. "Scenery talk. What's our next topic of conversation? The weather?"

"I like it up here," he said. "So does your mother. I think she'll be disappointed if it turns out we have to move."

173

"Move?" Okay, so now he had my attention. I looked up at him. He turned and stood beside me and peered out into the bush.

"I was at a conference in Toronto," he said. "On policing."

"For *five* days?" And if that was all it was, why hadn't Mom just said so? Why had she seemed so upset? And what was all this about moving?

"I was also checking out job opportunities," he said.

"But you just said — " Oh. If he and Mom didn't want to move, then there was only one reason I could think of why he was job-hunting. "It's Dave McDermott, isn't it? He's giving you a hard time."

"I had a performance review last week. Let's just say it didn't go as well as I had hoped."

"He didn't fire you, did he?"

"Not yet."

I didn't really want to ask the next question. I didn't want to hear the answer if it was going to turn out to be the one I was thinking. But how could I not ask?

"Does it have anything to do with Jonah Shackleton?"

"It has to do with a lot of things."

"One of which is Jonah Shackleton?"

He turned and looked down at me. "I guess it's fair to say that some people in town think Jonah's a bit of a troublemaker."

"Yeah, well, those must be the same people who thought Thomas Rennie was some kind of golden-boy hero," I said. Thomas was a local kid who had

174

stood by and let a member of his own football team drown. He hadn't even lifted a finger to help him. Nobody would ever have known if I hadn't stumbled onto the truth about Peter Flosnick's death . . .

Suddenly everything clicked into place.

"Is it *me*? Am I one of those lot of things?"

"No." He was looking me straight in the eye now; there was nothing evasive about him.

"Well, I bet you don't exactly earn bonus points because your — " I had been going to say daughter, but that wouldn't have been right because he wasn't my father. And, for some reason that I can't explain, I couldn't bring myself to say step-daughter, which is what I was. "Because I hang around with all the wrong people," I said instead.

"Dave McDermott is the kind of person who likes to be surrounded by yes-men," he said. "It makes him feel important to say something and have everyone else agree with him, even if they're only doing it because they depend on him. I've never been much of a yes-man."

"Me, neither," I said.

He grinned. "I know. That's one of the things I like about you. Now, come on, your mother should be just about ready to put supper on the table, and I don't know about you, but I'm hungry."

I didn't move. I looked up at him, trying to gauge his real mood. Then I said, "Norman Himmel wasn't where he was supposed to be the day that Mary Shackleton died."

The smile faded from his face. He peered down at me.

175

I told him what Ross and I had found out, and how we had found it out. His face grew more serious.

"You shouldn't be messing around in this," he said.

"But he had a motive. He was part of the consortium that wanted to develop the land."

Levesque shook his head. "Look, I know you and Jonah Shackleton have gotten to be friends — "

"This has nothing to do with that," I said angrily. "Jonah says his father didn't do it. You told me if I wanted to find out the truth, I should get out a shovel and start digging. Well, I did. And I found out that the other two partners in the consortium had an alibi for that morning, but that Norman Himmel didn't. Don't you think you should look into that?"

"Having no alibi doesn't make him a murderer."

"Having no alibi plus having a motive could do it, though," I said. "Imagine you were in East Hastings back then. Imagine this was your case. You'd check out everyone who might have had a motive, right, not just the most obvious person? You'd check out where everyone was, too, make sure they were where they said they were — "

"The Shackletons' door was locked," he reminded me.

"Maybe she let him in."

"The doors were all locked when Linda Shackleton got there. You need a key to lock them. No one outside of the family had a key. And no one saw anyone enter or leave the house that morning besides Harold Shackleton." He wasn't reciting all of this for my benefit, though. He was saying it all slowly, as if he were thinking it through for himself.

I waited a moment, then I said, "So, what are you going to do?"

He shrugged. "Whatever I do, *I* do."

I knew what he meant by that, and for the first time since I had met Jonah, I felt a little hope. He was telling me that he was going to look into it. He was telling me it was police business now.

"You hear me, Chloe?" he said.

I nodded. If it was police business, I wasn't supposed to go blabbing all over town about it. More specifically, I wasn't supposed to chatter about it to Jonah and Ross.

"Come on," he said. "Let's eat."

"I'll be there in a minute, okay?" I said.

He nodded.

I watched him lumber back up to the house, then I turned and looked out into the bush again. We hadn't lived up here for very long and if anyone had asked me where I considered home, I would still have said Montreal, where I was born and where I'd lived all my life until we moved here. So I was surprised to find myself angry at the thought of us having to move away from here. Funny, huh?

Chapter 14

Not showing up for class can make the total amount of time you spend in high school either longer than average, or shorter. In my opinion, being the oldest kid in his graduating class wouldn't do much to improve the quality of Jonah Shackleton's life. Neither would dropping out. So I made the rounds of his teachers, found out what work he had missed, and then headed over to his house after school.

No one answered when I rang the doorbell, but I didn't leave it at that. I knew his aunt was in town because I had walked by Stella's on the way to Jonah's and I had seen her standing behind the cash register. And judging from how Jonah had looked the other night, I was pretty sure that he hadn't strayed too far from home. So I rang the doorbell again and when that didn't get any results, I balled my hand into a fist and hammered on the front door.

"Come on, Jonah," I called, "open up. I'm not going away. I'm going to talk to you if I have to camp here until your aunt comes home from work."

A few moments later his face appeared in one of the three little windows set into the door.

"Go away," he said, his voice muffled by the thickness of the door.

I shook my head. "I brought your homework for

you. You're falling way behind, Jonah."

"I don't care."

"You will when everyone you know is graduating from university and you're still sitting in high school."

His faced vanished from sight.

"I am not leaving here until you open this door," I shouted. I hammered with both fists because now I was angry. I was doing him a favor. I had been helping him out all along. I was his friend, maybe the only one he had. How dare he shut me out like this!

Suddenly the door swung open and there stood Jonah, scowling at me. The eye that had been black and blue the last time I saw him was now streaked with green and yellow. A lot of the swelling had gone down, but it still looked painful. The scab on his lip was crusty and hard to look at. His sprained wrist was cradled in a sling. He reached out with his other hand.

"Give me the books and go," he said.

"Oh, please, you don't have to thank me, it was no trouble at all," I said as I wrestled my backpack off my back and crouched down on the cold porch to dig out his books. "What's an extra twenty pounds more or less strapped to my back?" Out came his math text, his history text, his French text. I slammed them down at his feet one by one. "There," I said, straightening up. I thrust the list of homework assignments at him. "If there's anything else I can do for you, don't bother to let me know."

"What's the matter with you?" Jonah said. "What

are you so mad about? I didn't ask you to come over here. I didn't ask for any favors."

"That's right, Jonah. You didn't. I decided to help you out all by myself. It's kind of like when someone decides to give you a present. They don't *have* to do it. They don't do it because you *asked* them to. They do it because they *like* you. When a friend decides to do something nice for you, you're not supposed to insult them or yell at them to go away. You're supposed to say thank you."

He just stared at me.

Fine.

I closed up my backpack and slung it over my shoulder.

"See you around," I said.

"I'm sorry," he said. Then he said, "Thank you."

"You're welcome," I snapped.

He didn't look angry any more. In fact, he looked sort of embarrassed.

"I'm sorry I yelled at you, Chloe. I know I'm being a jerk. You're on my side and I'm treating you like an enemy."

"It's okay."

"No, it's not."

Hey, I'm flexible. "Okay, you're right. It's not okay and you really are a jerk."

That's when a minor miracle happened. Jonah Shackleton smiled. I hadn't seen that happen more than maybe twice since I had known him.

"You want to come in?"

"I thought you'd never ask."

I followed him into the kitchen, where I was surprised to see that he was in the middle of making something.

"Peanut butter cookies," he said, a little sheepishly. "From my mother's recipe. For Jay. Just before the doorbell rang, I was finding out how hard it is to stir peanut butter and sugar together with just one good hand."

"You want some help?"

I picked up the wooden spoon that was on the counter and started to stir the sugar and peanut butter together. "You get out the ingredients and tell me what to do and I'll follow orders," I said. "How about that?"

"Well, it'll be a nice change of pace," he said.

I almost fell over with surprise. Jonah Shackleton actually had a sense of humor. I wondered what he would have been like if his mother hadn't died and if his father hadn't gone to prison.

"Okay, what else do we need?" I asked.

"Two eggs," he said, and handed them to me. I cracked them into the sugar and peanut butter.

"Beat together," Jonah said.

I started beating — and ended up with a glop of sugary peanut buttery egg on the front of my nearly new sweater. Jonah watched me rub at it to try to get it off.

"Maybe you should wear an apron," he said. He nodded to one hanging from a hook on the wall near the kitchen's back door. Beside the hook hung a piece of wood in the shape of a key. The wood was studded with little hooks, like cup hooks. Keys dangled from several of these.

"Great craftsmanship, huh?" Jonah said. "I made that for Aunt Linda back when I was in Cubs."

"Very cute," I said.

"It isn't supposed to be cute. It's supposed to be useful. You hang your keys up there and they don't get lost."

"I wasn't thinking of the key holder," I said. "I was thinking of you in a Cub uniform. Very cute."

He blushed. Jonah Shackleton actually blushed. Which made me grin. I slipped the neck loop of the apron over my head and knotted the ties around my waist.

For the next little while we worked together to mix up a batch of cookie dough. Then, when the first batch of cookies went into the oven, we both sat down and I said, "So, what happened the other day?"

Jonah shrugged. "A couple of guys decided to give me a hard time."

"Guys from school, you mean?"

He shook his head. "Just some guys."

"What guys? Did you tell the police who they are?"

He shook his head again.

"Why not? It looks like they beat you up pretty badly, Jonah. You could press charges."

"I don't want to."

"I could talk to Levesque. I could — "

"Forget it."

"But, Jonah — "

He stood up abruptly. "I don't want to go to the police. It wouldn't help."

182

"Why not? You know Levesque. He's a good guy."

"The three guys who beat me up — "

"Three?" I couldn't believe it. "Three guys against one? I hope they feel like some kind of heroes. You should definitely report them. Three against one isn't a fight. It's assault."

"It's my own fault," he said. "I fell for it."

"Fell for what?" What was he talking about?

"These guys started giving me a hard time. You know, how it was bad enough my mother refused to sell her land, how she didn't care that people up here need jobs, but for me to start saying my dad didn't do it and blaming the cops for my dad being in prison . . . I lost it. I shouldn't have, but I did."

"That doesn't make it your fault," I pointed out. "You could still press charges — "

"One of the guys is the son of the owner of Stella's. He works there as a busboy," Jonah said quietly. Grimly. "If I press charges and anything happens, it could be bad news for Aunt Linda."

"Yeah, but — "

"I don't want her to get fired on account of me."

"But — "

"I've made enough trouble for her, Chloe. I'm not going to make any more. No way."

I sighed. Okay. Time to back down. I hated to do it, but this wasn't my fight. Time to change the subject.

"How's Jay?"

Jonah shrugged. "He's been pretty quiet the past few days. I think Aunt Linda's worried."

"I was a little worried myself the other night," I admitted.

He frowned. "Why? What happened?"

"You know, the picture."

"What picture? What are you talking about?"

My turn to frown. I had been sure Linda would have told him about what had happened. But obviously she hadn't. Why not? Because she hadn't considered the incident significant enough to mention? Or for the opposite reason — that it was extremely significant, maybe even worrisome?

"Chloe?"

"It's nothing," I said.

Jonah peered at me. "You're not the kind of person who gets worried over nothing," he said. "What happened with Jay the other night?" When I still didn't say anything, he looked at me long and hard. "He's my brother," he said. "He's the closest family I have. Please tell me."

So I did. I told him about hearing a crash and then finding Jay standing in Linda's bedroom, broken glass all around him, just standing there, like he was in some kind of trance, as he tore a photograph into confetti-sized pieces.

"What photograph did you say it was?" Jonah asked when I had finished.

"It was in a silver frame. I think it must have been sitting on your aunt's dresser."

"A square silver frame?" he said. "With a little heart at the bottom?"

I thought for a moment. "Yes, I'm pretty sure." He nodded. "What?" I asked. "Who was in that picture?"

184

"Aunt Linda's ex-boyfriend."

I didn't get it. "Why would Jay shred a picture of your aunt's boyfriend?"

"Ex-boyfriend," he reminded me. "And he'd do it because he doesn't like the guy any more than I do."

I still didn't get it.

"Aunt Linda used to go out with Dave McDermott," Jonah said. "I don't know why she even kept that picture of him, after what he did. She was crazy about him. I remember hearing her and my mom talking one day. She was sure Dave was going to ask her to marry him. He didn't though. Instead, he dumped her right after my mother died." His voice was bitter with betrayal.

Jonah had already told me that his father and Dave had been friends. Now I understood that it had been more than that. Dave McDermott had been practically a member of the family. A member of the family who had sent Jonah's father to prison and who had broken his aunt's heart.

"No wonder you don't like the guy," I said.

The buzzer went off on the stove. Time to take the first batch of cookies out of the oven. I guess they were good cookies — that's what I told Jonah. I said, "Hey, who knew you'd have this kind of culinary talent." But I don't have any real memory of the cookies. I remember picking one up, I remember chewing it and complimenting Jonah, but I don't remember anything about how the cookie tasted. Mostly I was thinking about the sadness and disappointment and betrayal Jonah had suffered, and I felt sorry for him because it looked like it wasn't over yet. People weren't letting him forget. And it looked like Jonah was going to back down, for the sake of his aunt and his brother.

I wanted to tell him what I had told Levesque, but I had given Levesque my word. I wanted to say something that would make him feel better, that would give him hope. But I couldn't. Instead, after I ate that cookie and washed it down with a swig of milk, I did nothing. Nothing that made any difference, that is. I played a couple of hands of Old Maid with Jonah and Jay, I told Jonah I'd come back the next day and help him with the schoolwork he had missed, and then I went home to sit down to dinner with my own family, where everyone was alive and enjoying as much freedom as you can in this old world, and I never would have believed it, but I actually felt fortunate.

There was my mom, laughing and cooing at Shendor as she fed the dog bits of meat from her plate, despite Levesque's disapproval. "You're teaching her bad habits, Sheila," he said, to which my mother replied, "You didn't see her, Louis. She was cowering in the ditch. She was trembling. And she was starving." And there was Phoebe, rattling on about a one-act play she was directing in her drama class. At first I didn't listen to her. Then — I can't even say when I tuned in enough to notice it, but I did — Phoebe was not only excited about the play, but she was talking intelligently about it. If I hadn't been her sister, I would have thought, hey, that's interesting, that sounds like a good play that's being directed by someone who knows what she's talking about. And I thought, how did *that* happen? How did my kid sister go from being a snotty little brat to a, well, to an interesting and — was I running a fever or what? — a kind of attractive person?

And there was Levesque, chiding my mother about the dog, but not getting even remotely annoyed with her, and listening to Phoebe at the same time, nodding and commenting on what she was saying, all with this little smile tucked neatly under his moustache, so that there was no mistaking it, he was content. And I felt bad for Jonah all over again because he didn't have any of this.

I had just finished cleaning up the kitchen after supper when I heard my mother giggle. And because I heard her giggle, I wasn't surprised when she showed up in the kitchen to ask me if I would take Shendor for a walk when I had finished.

"Why can't Phoebe do it?" I said.

"Phoebe went back to school for a rehearsal." She made a pathetic please-please-please face.

"If you two want some time alone, why don't you both take the dog for a walk?" I said. And, yes, I knew that wasn't the kind of time alone they were looking for. "Okay," I said before she could start begging me again. "But I can't stay out all night. I have homework to do."

As soon as Mom handed me Shendor's leash, Shendor started barking and jumping up on me.

"Down, girl," I commanded. To my surprise, she sat immediately. She continued to sit, watching me, while I pulled on my jacket, but as soon as I started for the door, she jumped up and raced ahead of me. She was at the back door before I got there. I fastened the leash to the chain around her neck and pushed the door open. I thought I had a good grip on the leash. I know I was holding on to it. Apparently, though, I wasn't holding tightly enough because the minute Shendor got a snoutful of the crisp evening air, she started to run. And when she ran, she yanked the leash out of my hand. It trailed behind her as she raced down the slope of the backyard. The last I saw, she tore off into the bush at the end of our yard.

I could have gone straight back into the house and told my mother that I had just let her dog run away. I would have, too, if I had been desperate to spend the rest of the night feeling like the biggest disappointment of my mother's life. Instead, I decided to make a stab at redeeming myself, preferably without my mother ever knowing that I needed redemption. I locked the door behind me and hurried down the backyard after Shendor — hurried as fast as I could with an ankle that reminded me of its recent sprain every time I tried to run.

My motivations were good (I wanted to return my mother's beloved new pet) even if they weren't completely altruistic (I wanted to return the dog in order to avoid all sorts of punishment raining down on my head). You know that expression, about that road being paved with good intentions? Well, so is the road to accident and injury. Because all of this occurred *after* supper. In the dark, in other words.

And "in the dark" in a little town like East Hastings is nothing like "in the dark" in a big city like Montreal or Toronto. Once you get off the main street of East Hastings, there are no streetlights. In the bush that stretches to who knows where behind my house (at least, at the time I raced into it, my total knowledge of it was that it stretched to who knew where), the closest thing to light that you find is complete and utter darkness.

I stumbled a couple of times. A tree branch whipped me across the face, and, trust me, that sounds funny only up to the point when it actually happens to you, and then you aren't laughing. Finally I stopped in my tracks and thought, you are one crazy person, Chloe. For all I knew, there could be bears in this bush. Or coyotes. Or other nibbly critters.

I stopped, panting, and looked around and realized that I couldn't see anything that didn't look like a tree. This is not a comforting realization for someone who is, essentially, an urban creature. Don't panic, I told myself. I had entered the bush on a path and, so far as I could tell, I was still on some sort of path. I stood still and breathed in the cool evening air. Gradually my eyes grew accustomed to the gloom. Yes, I did seem to be on some sort of path. All I had to do was retrace my steps . . .

Uh-oh. Something was out there. A creature. My heart stopped in my chest. What if it really was a nibbly critter? What if it suddenly leapt at me, fangs bared, aimed for my throat? What if . . .

Oh, puh-lease. What were the chances?

"Shendor?" I called softly. "Shendor, is that you?"

"Arf!" replied Shendor.

I took a step toward her. "Good girl, Shendor," I said. "Good girl. Sit, Shendor."

At which point Shendor bounded even deeper into the bush, and I — what else could I do? — I followed.

I fell twice — do you have any idea how treacherous tree roots can be? — and I got slapped in the face by a couple more branches. But it wasn't a complete loss, because Shendor seemed to find the whole chase enormously entertaining. She made a game of it. She would race so far into the bush that she would disappear from sight, I would stumble after her until yet another tree attacked me, and then, just as I was cursing nature, I would catch sight of Shendor, an inky spot way ahead in the distance. She would "arf" at me again and she'd sit there until I had just about convinced myself that *this* time I was going to be able to grab her, then off she'd go.

Here's something I never would have known if I had not played this little game with Shendor: Humans get tired of chasing dogs a whole lot sooner than dogs get tired of being chased. I was so mad with both myself and her that I lost track of how far into the bush I had gone or how or whether I was going to manage to get back to where I had started. All I wanted was to get my hands around Shendor. That was when, of course, she vanished completely.

"Shendor?" I called.

No reassuring "arf" greeted me.

"Shendor? Good dog." Yeah, right. If she was a good dog, she (a) wouldn't have run away, and (b) would have come when I called her. I thought about my mother finding her by the side of the road and wondered just who had abandoned whom. "Shendor, where are you?"

When I still didn't hear her and couldn't see any dog-shaped smudge of darkness up ahead, I started to panic, and not because I was worried about what my mother was going to say if I returned dog-less. I was thinking about how she would react if I never returned at all. I turned around to look at where I had just come from. Okay, I know, I'm such a city girl it's pathetic. But I was scared. It was creepy in that bush. I turned around again and wondered which way to go — back or forward. Shendor had to be up ahead somewhere. She was probably waiting just out of sight, and suddenly I longed for her reassuring presence, even if she remained beyond reach. I started forward again, stumbling, angry, scared. And then I saw a light. Just a small light, like a star hanging low to the horizon. Except that, unlike a star, it seemed to get bigger the farther forward I went. Then two things happened all at once. First, I saw Shendor quite clearly, sitting up ahead, with not a single tree around her. She was in some sort of clearing. And second, I realized that the star was, in fact, the light from a window. I had reached the other end of the bush.

As I crept toward Shendor, she stood up. But she

didn't run away. She just stood there, her tail flicking back and forth faster than a metronome doing six-eight time. This time when I was within grasping distance of her, she ran toward me, and when I knelt down to grab her leash, she leapt up and licked my face. Normally I hate doggy slobber, but I was so happy to have that leash wrapped securely around my hand that I didn't care. When I stood up I saw that the path continued along the edge of the clearing. Then I looked at that window in the distance and I saw a person. She was standing there full in the window, gazing out, not at me — I don't think she could see me — but at the night. Her head was tilted up a little, as if she were staring at the sky. It was Linda Shackleton. Using the roads, her house was a good half-hour walk from mine. But following a straight line — "as the crows fly," Levesque would have said — it was a whole lot closer.

Chapter 15

It's funny how things go. When you're just starting out to do something, even when you think that actually accomplishing that something is going to be a long shot, you have hope. You think, *maybe* it's possible. After all, people are always telling you, "Anything is possible."

When I first decided to look into whether Harold Shackleton could conceivably be innocent, I was hoping that I could help an angry person I barely knew come to terms with a bad situation in his life. But as I poked around and got to know Jonah, what I hoped for shifted. Gradually I started to hope that maybe I would find something that might get Harold Shackleton out of prison. Yes, I know. What would make me think that I could find something that everyone from police officers to lawyers to judges and juries had missed? But hope is like that. A lot of people hope for a lot of crazy things. They don't necessarily share their secret yearnings and wishes with the whole world — life is tough enough without everyone telling you, "It can't be done," without them stealing the little stick of hope that might be the only thing keeping you afloat.

Now, though, I had done everything I could, except wait. Wait for Levesque to dig around a little, if that was what he was doing. Wait for him to maybe find something — or maybe not find anything at all. Maybe it was like he said — no alibi doesn't necessarily equate with murderer. I thought the waiting was going to drive me crazy.

All through the next day at school, whenever I had a break, I checked with Jonah's teachers to collect homework assignments for him. Madame Benoit asked me if I knew when he was coming back to school.

"Je ne sais pas," I told her. I was beginning to think that even Jonah didn't have the answer to that one.

Ross caught up with me at my locker after school.

"You haven't been down at the newspaper office for days," he complained.

I said nothing — what was there to say? — and continued to stuff textbooks into my backpack.

"Don't you have anything to tell me?" Ross asked.

"Like what?"

"You missed this week's deadline, Chloe. I didn't have anything to fill the space. I had to stay up half the night writing a story so I wouldn't have three empty columns on page five."

"I'm sorry, Ross. I've been busy."

"With Jonah, right?" Even though I knew he felt a little differently about Jonah now, he still seemed to have trouble saying his name without giving it a twist of disapproval. "What's happening now? Did you tell your stepdad?"

"I told him," I said. "And, nothing."

"He's looking into it, though, right?"

"I'm not supposed to talk about it, Ross."

Ross nodded. "Yeah, he's looking into it."

I yanked on my backpack drawstring and tied it shut, then I closed my locker. "I'll get my article in for the next issue, I promise," I told him.

* * *

I'm not one hundred percent positive, but I think Jonah was happy to see me. He even seemed to be waiting for me. The front door opened just as I was reaching for the doorbell.

"How's the arm?" I asked.

"Sore."

"Madame Benoit wants to know when you're coming back to school."

"As soon as Jay is better," he said.

"What's the matter with him?" A picture flashed in my mind of Jay with his arm in a sling. "Is he hurt?"

"Sick," Jonah said. "He was complaining of a stomachache this morning. Aunt Linda didn't want to call in sick. She's already missed some days in the past couple of weeks. So I told her I'd stay home until he was feeling better. I also promised to keep up with my schoolwork. I don't want her to worry any more than she already does."

I remembered what I had thought about Jonah the first time I met him. Boy, had I ever been wrong.

"Well then," I said, "let's get busy. You've missed a lot of work, and exams are coming up."

We settled down at the dining room table and started in on French review. We had just finished that and were going on to history when Jay called from upstairs.

"I feel like I'm gonna throw up," he wailed.

Jonah sighed and headed for the stairs. I followed. Just as we reached the top, we heard a terrible gagging sound. Then the smell reached us. When we got to Jay's room, he was sitting up in bed in a puddle of vomit. He was crying.

Jonah turned and looked apologetically at me. I smiled and shrugged.

"You get him into the bathtub and then into some clean pajamas," I said. "I'll strip his bed and get everything into the washing machine."

Five minutes later, I was down in Linda Shackleton's back porch laundry room, measuring out laundry detergent. Twenty minutes after that, Jonah was back downstairs with Jay, who looked pale, but clean and sweet-smelling in a fresh pair of Star Wars flannel pajamas. Jay did not look pleased to see me.

"He wants to know what you've done with Mr. Edgar."

"Mr. Edgar?"

"His bear," Jonah explained.

Ah. "Mr. Edgar had throw-up on him," I said directly to Jay. "I had to put him in the washing machine."

Jay's face scrunched up and grew very red. "I want him back. Give him back right now."

He was so angry that I looked to Jonah for an explanation. Jonah only shrugged.

"You can have him back as soon as he's washed and dried," I said. "He was all smelly, Jay."

Just then the washing machine buzzed to let me know that it had finished its cycle. I scooped everything out of it and stuffed it all into the dryer.

"It'll be less than an hour," I told Jay. "I promise."

Jay sat down on the floor in front of the dryer and refused to budge. He was going to wait until Mr. Edgar emerged safe and dry, and that was that. Jonah finally gave up and wrapped his little brother in a blanket so he wouldn't catch a chill.

"When the dryer is finished, it'll buzz," he told Jay. "Call us when it does and we'll get Mr. Edgar for you. Okay?"

Jay nodded solemnly.

Jonah and I went back into the dining room.

"I feel like I just committed the crime of the century," I said to Jonah.

"Mr. Edgar has never been washed." He kept his voice low so that Jay wouldn't hear. "Aunt Linda tried to wrestle it away from him a hundred times. She finally gave up when Jay told her Mr. Edgar smelled like Mom."

I slumped back in my chair.

"I'm sorry, Jonah," I said. "But what could I do? There was throw-up on him."

"It's okay," Jonah said. "Aunt Linda would have done the same thing under the circumstances."

He opened his textbook and we moved from history to chemistry. At least, he did. I had trouble concentrating. Eventually the dryer buzzed. When we got to it, Jay had already opened the door and was pawing frantically through the clothes.

"He's not here," he cried.

"Sure, he is," I said. "I put him in myself." I nudged him aside and burrowed into the warm clean sheets and pillowcases until I felt a fleecy little arm. "Got him," I said, and pulled him free. "Uh-oh," I said, and realized right away that it would have been better to think it rather than say it out loud.

"What uh-oh?" Jay said, his eyes growing wide with concern.

Mr. Edgar must have been older than I thought, because one of his seams had split in the washing machine and some of his stuffing was leaking out.

"Nothing I can't fix with a needle and thread," I said. I studied Mr. Edgar's wound a little more closely. The little tail-ends of thread where the seam had split were a different color from the thread around it. Mr. Edgar had apparently undergone surgery at least once before. I looked to Jonah for help.

"I'll get Aunt Linda's sewing basket," he said, and hurried upstairs, leaving me alone with Jay, who now had tears dribbling down his cheeks.

"Don't worry," I told him. "He just needs a few stitches and then he'll be as good as new." I showed him the spot that I planned to mend. "I'll be very careful. You won't even be able to see the stitches when I'm done.

He didn't look convinced, but he nodded and followed me into the dining room. I pulled a chair close to mine so that he could sit beside me and watch what I was doing. Then I hunted through Linda's sewing basket for some caramel brown thread and a needle.

"Okay," I said, after I threaded the needle, "here we go." I picked up the bear and stuck the needle into him. Beside me, Jay let out a yelp, so that I dropped Mr. Edgar and stuck myself in the finger.

"What's the matter?" Jonah asked.

"Mr. Edgar doesn't like needles," Jay said.

"*You* don't like needles," Jonah pointed out. "Mr. Edgar isn't afraid of them. He knows this needle is going to help him. He's not even the least bit scared."

I sucked my stuck finger for a moment, then bent down to retrieve poor Mr. Edgar. As my hand closed around him I felt something hard and sharp inside, just as I had the time I had sat on him. I felt again. Whatever was in there was a hazard to a little kid. I worked the hard object toward the split side seam and worked it out. I don't know what I had expected the object to be, but I was surprised by what I ended up holding in my hand.

"Where did this come from?" I asked, and held the object out on the palm of my hand so that both Jay and Jonah could see it.

"What is it?" Jonah asked.

"It's a button," I said, and peered at it. "It looks like — "

Jay snatched the button from my hand.

"It's mine," he said. He closed his hand around it.

"It looks like a uniform button," I said. I couldn't imagine what it was doing inside a stuffed animal.

"Maybe it got in there by mistake at the factory," Jonah said.

"I don't see how," I said, "unless Mr. Edgar was made in a factory run by the army. It's a brass button, like the kind you see on military uniforms."

Jonah looked surprised. He turned to his brother. "Let me see it, Jay."

Jay shook his head and hid his fist behind his back.

"Come on, Jay, I just want to take a look at it. I'll give it right back, I promise."

Jay shook his head again. He looked like he was going to start crying again.

Jonah looked completely baffled by this. "What's the matter, Jay-Jay?" he said. "Don't you trust me?"

When Jay shook his head again, Jonah reacted as if he had just been punched in the stomach. Hard.

"Hey, Jay, it's me. We're brothers, right? We stick together, right? If you can't trust your own brother, who can you trust?"

"But you said . . . " Jay's voice trailed off.

"I said what?"

"You threw away all the newspapers. You got rid of all the pictures. You made Aunt Linda get rid of everything."

I had no idea what he was talking about, but I could see that Jonah understood. His own face went pale and his eyes got all watery. For a moment, I thought he was going to cry.

"I didn't get rid of anything," he said. "I wanted to." He looked at me. "I went a little nuts after Mom . . . I didn't want anything around that reminded me of her." He reached out with his good hand and caught Jay under the chin and tilted his head up so that he had no choice but to look at Jonah. "I wanted to get rid of her things, Jay, but Aunt Linda talked me out of it. She put everything away for us. The pictures, Mom's stuff, everything. You can see it all anytime you want to. I'll call Aunt Linda right now, if you want, and ask her where she put everything."

Jay nodded. His face was wet with tears now, and his lower lip trembled when he said, "Yes, please." Then he opened his small fist and handed the button to Jonah. "I kept this," he said. "I feel it in Mr. Edgar and it makes me remember Mommy."

Jonah peered down at the brass button and then looked across the top of Jay's head at me. I knew exactly what he was thinking — why would a button make him think of his mother?

"Where did you get this, Jay?" Jonah asked.

What he told us was a surprise.

"Are you *sure?*" Jonah kept asking. After all, Jay was only two years old at the time. "Are you positive?"

Jay nodded.

That trembling little nod led to a whole lot of other questions, one of which led us to Aunt Linda.

* * *

By the time Jonah's Aunt Linda got home from work, Jay was sound asleep in his bed. She looked alarmed when we told her that he had thrown up, but relaxed again when Jonah reported that we had taken his temperature only thirty minutes ago and that it was close to normal. She slumped down onto the couch in the living room without even tak-

201

ing off her coat. Jonah glanced at me, and then sat down beside her.

"Aunt Linda, can we ask you something?"

Two little worry lines appeared between her eyes. She was probably wondering what the question would be, but she nodded.

"It's about that morning," he said. He didn't have to say what morning. I could tell from the way Linda Shackleton's shoulders slumped that she knew. She knew and she wished the whole subject would go away.

"Jonah, I thought we agreed not to talk about this any more," she said. She didn't sound angry, though. Mostly she sounded tired. Then she sighed. "Okay, what is it?"

Jonah took a deep breath and then asked, "Was there anyone in the house with you that morning when Mom called?"

For a split second Linda Shackleton looked confused. Then she looked startled. Then her expression changed to something else, something that made me worry.

"What's this all about, Jonah?" she said.

Jonah must have picked up on her expression, too, because he immediately said, "We're not accusing you of anything, Aunt Linda." Then, "But you and Dave were practically engaged, and Norman Himmel was one of the partners in the North Mines project and he was Dave's brother-in-law — "

"Brother-in-law to be," Aunt Linda corrected. "Susan and Norm had just started going out together."

"Was Dave McDermott here the morning Mom died?" Jonah asked.

At first Linda Shackleton was so still that I thought she hadn't heard the question. Then, slowly, she nodded. A tear leaked from one of her eyes.

"He told me not to worry," she said to Jonah. "I told him what your mother said when she called, that she had just told your father that she was planning to sign over the land to that environmental group. I told him that she and your father had been fighting and that I was afraid something might happen. But Dave told me not to worry. He said couples argue all the time. Then he got into his car and drove away to do his rounds."

I thought of all the newspaper articles I had read. "You never mentioned at the trial that he had been at your house that morning," I said as gently as I could.

"He asked me not to. He said, 'How would it look, the police saying there was nothing to worry about and the next thing you know, someone is murdered.' After — " She sniffled and I handed her some tissues. "Afterwards, Dave and I fought about it. I think I blamed him for not going over there that morning. Maybe if he had, things would have turned out differently."

Maybe, I thought. But I doubted it.

"Did anyone call Dave when he was here?" I asked.

She shook her head.

"Are you sure?" I pressed. "Nobody called and asked for him?"

"Nobody called at all except Mary," Linda Shackleton said.

* * *

I don't know why I thought Ross would need convincing, but the truth was, he didn't. He showed up the next morning exactly when I asked him to — after Phoebe had gone to a friend's, Mom was grocery shopping and Levesque was at the office. And now here we were, standing out on my street in the cold. I had taken up a position halfway up the driveway of our nearest neighbor on one side of my house. Ross was standing like a sentinel partway up the driveway of our nearest neighbor on the other side. Anyone watching us would have wondered why we weren't in school. The more paranoid might have wondered what we were up to.

I fought the urge to look at Ross, and kept my eyes squarely on my house. From where I was standing, I had a pretty good view of the whole front of it, and an excellent view of the east side of it. Ross had the west side covered. I wondered if his toes were as cold as mine. The temperature had dropped during the night. I stamped my feet as I stood there waiting.

And waiting.

And waiting.

Then, movement.

The front door to my house opened and someone — Jonah — stepped out onto the front porch. He waved at me. I checked my watch, waved back, then started toward him.

"So?" Jonah said when I was close enough that he

didn't have to shout. "Did you see me?"

I shook my head. I had been staring at the house the whole time, and I hadn't seen him until he opened the front door.

I looked over at Ross. "What about you?" I asked.

Ross shook his head. "I didn't see a thing."

Jonah turned back to me. "Now what?" he asked.

Chapter 16

If real life were like the movies, every Christmas would be a white Christmas, it would never get so cold on Halloween that little kids had to cover their costumes with parkas, every person in a hurry would find a parking space when they needed one, and three kids could put a murderer away for life just like that, no problem.

But life isn't like the movies, and even though we were holding a lot of the pieces, we couldn't finish assembling the puzzle. We needed help. Time to call the cops.

Jonah and Ross and I trudged down to the police station. Levesque was on the phone and stayed on it for a good long time, even though I used all the body language I could muster to get the message across that I had something important to talk to him about. When he finally hung up we told him everything we had found out — how someone could have gotten into the Shackleton house without being seen, how someone else outside of the Shackleton family had access to a key to the house and could have locked the door before Linda Shackleton had showed up, and what we thought had happened.

If life were like the movies, Levesque would have gotten up out of his chair immediately, he would have called to Officer Steve Denby and the two of

206

them would have gone out and made an arrest or two. We would have been instant heroes, Harold Shackleton would have been freed from prison, and all the Shackletons would have lived happily ever after.

But life isn't like the movies.

Levesque listened carefully to everything we told him. He asked a few questions. When he finally got up out of his chair, it was only to thank us for coming and to walk us to the door.

"Aren't you going to do something?" I asked.

"I'll look into what you've told me," he said. "And I'd appreciate it if, in the meantime, you would keep everything under your hats."

"Are you going to take this seriously?" I said. "Or is this a brush-off?"

"I said I'd look into it."

"But — "

"I'll keep you posted," he said, which, experience had taught me, could be roughly translated as, "If any arrests are made, you'll eventually find out about it."

We left the police station in silence. Jonah gave me a what-did-I-tell-you? look. And then . . . nothing happened.

A day passed. Then another and another. Ross drove me crazy asking me what was going on. Jonah didn't say a word. His silence was worse than Ross's million and one questions.

Four days after we had told him everything we had found out, Levesque didn't show up for supper. Mom said he was working late. That same evening

I listened to a local newscast while I was cleaning up the kitchen. The Liberal Party was holding its nomination meeting the next night. Dave McDermott was considered the only serious contender, the announcer said, a shoo-in for the nomination. If I had been cleaning up my own dishes instead of Mom's, I would have smashed them all, one by glorious one, that's how angry I was. I decided to wait up for Levesque. He owed me an explanation for why he had done nothing.

I heard the front door open a little after midnight. Mom was already asleep — she had pulled another double shift at the Canadian Tire store where she worked, which meant she had been on her feet for twice as long as she usually was. Phoebe was in bed too. By the time I got to the front hall, Levesque was bent over, untying his bootlaces. He set his boots neatly against the foyer wall and came inside in sock feet.

"You're up late for a school night." he said as he pulled off his sheepskin jacket and hung it in the hall closet.

"I want to know what's going on."

He closed the closet door and brushed by me on his way to the kitchen. When I caught up with him again, he was peering into the fridge. I waited while he pulled out a couple of eggs, some cheese, the butter.

"You said you'd look into what we told you," I said.

All he was looking into was the cupboard beside the oven, more intent on locating the frying pan than on listening to me. He found it, set it on the stove and pulled a small bowl from another cupboard. He cracked the eggs into it. As he beat them with a fork he said, "I did."

This was news. "And?"

"And things take time. This isn't television, you know." He set the bowl down and cut a small piece of butter, which he dropped into the frying pan. While that melted, he grated some cheese.

"You haven't found out anything?" I said.

He shot me a look — *the* look, the one that was meant to warn me that I was crossing the line. Pressing him to talk about police work was inadvisable, as he never tired of telling me. I shook my head. I was in no mood for his going-by-the-book routine.

"Don't give me that," I said. "You wouldn't be looking into anything if it wasn't for me. I'm the one who told you that Norman Himmel had a motive for killing Mary Shackleton and no alibi for the time of the murder. I'm also the one who found the button. And if that button was in Mary Shackleton's hand when she died" — that's what Jay had told us, that's why he had kept it, because he thought it was hers — "then that proves that Dave McDermott was in the house *before* she died, which meant he was there before Linda Shackleton showed up. The only reason he could have been there is that Norman Himmel got himself into big trouble and he called his pal Dave to bail him out. Which Dave did, by pinning the murder on Harold Shackleton to keep suspicion away from Norman

Himmel."

Levesque gave me a hard look that worked on my confidence the way a jackhammer works on cement.

"Norman Himmel hit Mary Shackleton over the head, pushed her down the basement stairs, and then called the police to bail him out?" he said.

Even I had to admit that when he put it that way . . .

"Why would he do something like that?" he said. "And why would Dave McDermott agree to help him?" He stared at me, waiting for an answer. I felt like the one kid in class who hadn't done her homework, but who had been sent to the blackboard to produce an answer.

"Himmel and McDermott were old friends," I said.

"If an old friend of mine murdered someone and then called me for help, what do you suppose I would do?"

He was making my theory look like two plus two equals three-and-a-half.

"Think about it," Levesque went on. "According to what you're saying, Mary Shackleton had to have been alive when McDermott arrived. If she was and if McDermott did nothing, he was implicating himself in a murder. Why would he do that, even for an old friend?"

"Maybe she died right after he got there. Maybe there was nothing he could have done to save her anyway."

He made a sour face. "Pass me a couple of slices

210

of bread, would you?"

I felt like throwing the whole loaf at him.

He popped the bread into the toaster, then poured the egg mixture into the frying pan, where it started to sizzle.

"Maybe Himmel had something on McDermott. Maybe he was blackmailing him," I said. Hey, it even sounded good. "That would explain why McDermott didn't turn him in."

"I don't suppose you have any theories on what Himmel was using to blackmail him?"

No, I didn't.

The toast popped up in the toaster. Levesque took out both slices, buttered them, and set them on a plate. Then he folded over his omelet and slid it onto the plate, too.

"Pour me a glass of milk, would you?" he said as he carried his food into the dining room.

I sloshed some milk into a glass and followed him.

He shook some salt and pepper on his omelet, took a bite, and sighed. I guessed it had been a long day. I waited. When he finally spoke again, he said, "I shouldn't be telling you this, so I'm going to make you promise that this stays between the two of us."

I promised.

"I had a chat with the Crown today," he said. He meant the crown attorney responsible for this jurisdiction.

"And?"

"And there are big problems."

"Like?"

"Well, for one thing, the fact that the only information we have comes from someone who was barely two years old at the time. Jay Shackleton's memory of what happened that day is hardly reliable. It definitely wouldn't be admitted in court."

Strike one.

"What about the button?" I said. "It came off a police uniform, didn't it?"

"It appears to have," Levesque said.

"Well, doesn't that put Dave McDermott at the scene of the crime?"

"*If* it belongs to Dave McDermott, yes, it puts him in the house — at some point. But — " How did I know there was going to be a *but*? "Dave McDermott was the investigating officer. It's no secret that he was in the house shortly after the murder. A number of people saw him there. He could have lost the button then."

"But Jay said — " I broke off. Jay wasn't reliable. He had been too young. And, sure as he might sound, even I had to concede that it would be impossible to convict anyone of anything on the strength of what a two-year-old said. This wasn't working out the way I had hoped.

"I don't suppose anyone remembers exactly what Dave McDermott was wearing that day," I said. I did realize, of course, that the day in question was over five years ago.

Levesque took another hearty bite of egg.

"The coroner remembers uniform pants and shirt," he said. "No jacket."

"Which means . . . "

"It could mean a couple of things. It could mean that Dave removed his jacket because he was feeling warm."

"Or that he noticed one of the buttons was missing, but he didn't want anyone else to notice," I said.

Levesque shrugged. "How about this for a theory?" he said. I pricked up my ears, expecting a brilliant solution. Instead I got, "Jay is mistaken about the button. He picked it up after McDermott was there. Maybe he even got it from his Aunt Linda's house. Maybe he associates it with his mother for some reason that isn't even valid. He wasn't much more than a baby at the time and he was pretty traumatized by what happened."

This was definitely not going according to plan.

"So you're writing off the button?" I said.

He didn't say anything, which I took as a yes.

"What about Norman Himmel?" I asked. "Did you check him out? Does anyone know where he was that morning?"

The phone rang before he could answer. Levesque grabbed the receiver on the second ring and listened grimly to whoever was on the other end. When he hung up he headed straight for the closet and snagged his jacket.

"What's up?" I asked, watching him shove his feet into his boots.

"Jay Shackleton is missing."

I felt like someone had kicked me in the stomach.

"What do you mean, missing?"

"His aunt came home from an evening out. She went into his room and he wasn't there. He isn't anywhere in the house. Jonah says he didn't hear him leave. He may have been gone for an hour or he may have been gone all evening. Tell your mother where I've gone."

"Can I come with you?"

"I have to check things out, Chloe," he said. "If we can't find him, we may have to mobilize a search party. I'll let you know."

I shivered when he opened the door and stepped out into the night. My breath hung like a cloud in the cold night air. Wherever Jay had gone, I sure hoped he had dressed warmly.

Chapter 17

The phone rang at six o'clock the next morning. Mom got to it before I could. I heard her talking softly into the receiver, then I heard her call, "Chloe, Phoebe!"

She was sitting up in bed when we got to her.

"Get dressed," Mom said. She swung her legs out of bed. "And put on warm clothes."

"What's up?" Phoebe asked. "Did the furnace break down at school?"

"You're not going to school this morning," Mom said. "Jay Shackleton is missing. A search party is being put together."

I felt sick to my stomach. Levesque had left hours ago, which meant that Jay had been missing hours longer than that. I hurried to put on some warm clothes. Mom met us downstairs with peanut butter on toast, which we ate as she drove us down to the police station.

Levesque was outside, the collar of his sheepskin coat pulled up around his neck. His face looked gray. He had been up all night. Dozens of people were milling around on the sidewalk. I saw Jonah and Linda Shackleton among them. Their faces were pale. Linda Shackleton had been crying. Then I saw Dave McDermott wading into the crowd toward her. She started to turn away from him, but when he said something to her that I couldn't hear, she collapsed against him and he held her in his arms. Jonah walked away from them in disgust. I headed to where he was standing, but before I could reach him, someone grabbed my arm.

"What are you trying to do to me?" Norman Himmel hissed. I was so surprised to see him here that at first I couldn't think of anything to say. "Why are you asking everyone questions about me? Why are you trying to ruin my reputation?"

I jerked free of his grip, but he came toward me again. I darted through the crowd toward Levesque, who was trying to get everyone to be quiet so that he could give instructions.

Levesque and Steve Denby divided us into groups. Some people were going to search every nook and cranny in town. Some were being dispatched to look for Jay out of town. I was assigned to the western entrance of East Hastings Provincial Park. I looked for Jonah, to get him to come with me, but I didn't see him anywhere. I headed off to the park with my group and then we all split up.

For the first little while, I could see some of the others who had been assigned to the park with me. But after a while, they faded off into the distance. The park was big and there wasn't a month that went by that some tourist didn't get lost in it. Steve Denby had given everyone a photocopied map of the park and a section to search and we were all told to stick to marked trails. Good thing, too, because I didn't want Levesque to have to send a search party out after me too.

My method was pretty much like everyone else's — I walked slowly down the trail in my assigned area and called Jay's name at intervals. Called and got no answer. When I stopped calling, I could hear other voices, but they were all saying the same thing I was. "Jay! Jay Shackleton! Are you there, Jay?"

No answer.

I'm not sure when I realized that I wasn't hearing other voices any more. It didn't bother me, though, because, ta-dah!, I had a map. I was walking and looking at it and calling Jay's name and pausing and listening for an answer, when all of a sudden I saw a flash of red darting down a ravine up ahead. I hurried toward it and came to a grinding halt when the ground suddenly dropped off ahead of me. I peered down into the ravine and saw the flash of red again, disappearing in the distance.

"Jay!" I called. "Jay, is that you?"

No answer. The patch of red vanished. A narrow trail led down into the ravine. It was a foot and a half wide at most — and it dropped off sharply on the side farthest from the ravine wall. Immediately below were rock outcroppings — glacial deposits, my geography textbook would have called them — and, beyond and below them, an icy stream. I hurried down the trail as quickly as I could, scanning the woods at the bottom for any sign of that patch of red.

Big mistake.

When you're in the woods, you should always watch your feet. Why? Because it reduces your chances of tripping over a rock or a log or a length of tree root. It was a tree root that got me, a thick loop that came out of the earth on one side of the trail and disappeared into it again on the other side, just before it dropped off altogether. I didn't see it and, as a result, caught my foot in it and went flying forward. Well, part of me went flying forward. My foot remained caught in the root, and when I finally hit the ground, I heard something snap. Somehow, I didn't think it was the tree root. I struggled to my feet. Correction, attempted to struggle. Second correction, to my foot, not feet, because my ankle screamed when I tried to put any weight on it. Let them try and tell me at the hospital that it wasn't broken this time.

So, what do you do when you're out in a search party trying to find a lost seven-year-old who probably knows the place you're searching like the back of his hand because he's lived here all his life and you haven't and you fall and probably — make that definitely — break your stupid ankle?

You yell for help.

I did, and when I didn't get an answer, it really sank in that it had been a while since I had heard anyone calling Jay's name. For all I knew, he was safely back in town and now I was the one who was lost.

I yelled again, but no one yelled back. No one called to me to hang on, help was on the way. The damsel in distress routine wasn't working. Time to pull myself up by my own bootstraps, as my grade eight history teacher used to say. I started to make my way back up to the top of the ravine. Here's something I learned that day: It's a whole lot harder to hop up a steep, narrow trail than it is to trip your way down it. Every step — hop — forward was paid for by a yelp of genuine pain. Then, suddenly, a face appeared above me like a moon rising in a clear sky.

"Well, well," Norman Himmel said, peering down at me, "what happened here?"

I tried to fight back the creepy panicky feeling that filled my stomach and made me want to throw up. Instead, I pretended he didn't scare me to death. I said, "I could use some help."

"Could you?" he said. "Why would I want to help you after you've been going around asking people all kinds of questions about me?"

Lois at the veterinary clinic must have said something about our visit. Ditto Ms. Henderson with the breakfast program at the school. But we had been asking about the day Mary Shackleton died. We hadn't specifically asked about Norman Himmel's whereabouts, so it sounded to me like somebody had a guilty conscience. Somebody standing over me. The only person around who could actually help me.

Then I heard another voice.

"Hey, Norm, what's going on?"

Dave McDermott's voice. Just great. A moment later he appeared beside Norman Himmel and peered down at me the way a wild animal might examine a small defenseless creature it had firmly gripped in its claws.

I looked up at both of them and shouted again for help.

Dave McDermott shook his head.

"I guess you didn't hear," he said. "I just got the call myself." He held up his cell phone. "Little Jay is safe and sound back in town. The search has been called off."

"Terrific," I said, but, to tell the truth, I felt anything but terrific. In fact, I felt almost sick to my stomach because of the pain. The gruesome twosome peering down at me didn't improve the situation. I wanted to get out of the ravine and to somewhere where someone would give me something to make the pain go away. "You want to help me out of here?"

Dave McDermott glanced at his brother-in-law. Then I saw him look behind me. I twisted around and looked, too. There were only a few inches between me and where the trail dropped off. Directly below that were all those nice glacially deposited rocks.

"A person could have a nasty fall," Dave McDermott said.

"And a person could find himself in a lot of trouble if anything were to happen to me because of anything he did or didn't do," I said. Sounding, I hoped, really tough. Feeling about as tough as a pair of ballet slippers in a crowd of steel-toed construction boots. "If something happens to me, Levesque will find out," I said, to make sure he got my point. "It won't look good for your political career." Then, I don't know what came over me, I was mad, I guess, and I can't help myself when I get mad, "Neither will covering for your brother-in-law."

Norman Himmel surprised me by looking surprised himself.

"What is she talking about?" he said to Dave McDermott.

Dave McDermott batted at the air with a wave of annoyance. "She's not talking about anything."

Oh, wasn't she?

"There was a witness," I told Norman Himmel. "Someone was there. Someone saw what happened. That's why I was asking all those questions. My father" — it sounded a little closer and, therefore, a little more threatening than stepfather, at least I hoped it did — "is looking into it."

Sweat glistened on Himmel's forehead and upper lip, but it couldn't have been from the heat of the day because there wasn't any heat. I was shaking with cold. Or maybe with shock.

"What is she talking about, a witness?" he demanded of Dave McDermott. "There's no witness."

"Shut up," McDermott said.

Himmel could shut up if he wanted to, but I couldn't. I didn't like Dave McDermott and didn't trust him. The way I saw it, my best chance to get out of the ravine in one un-splattered piece was to convince Norm Himmel that hurting me was only going to hurt him more in the long run.

"Someone was in the house when Mary Shackleton died," I said. "Someone saw the whole thing."

Himmel's face loomed larger and closer over me. "What are you saying?"

"Someone saw you in the house. Someone saw what you did."

"Don't listen to her," McDermott said. "She doesn't know what she's talking about."

I glanced at McDermott. "I guess you didn't tell him about the button you lost, huh?"

"Button?" Himmel said. "What button?"

"The button that was found in Mary Shackleton's hand," I said. "The button that has McDermott's DNA on it." Well, maybe it would have if I hadn't sent it through the washing machine. "They can prove it, you know. You've seen how he polishes his buttons. Mr. Spit-and-Polish, isn't that what they call him? He was wearing his uniform that day, wasn't he, Mr. Himmel? He was wearing it and just before she died, she grabbed him, isn't that how it happened? She grabbed him and pulled off a button, only he didn't notice, he was too busy thinking how he could get you out from under a murder charge, how he could make it look like Harold Shackleton did it, not you."

"Don't listen to her," McDermott said. "She's a kid. She's a friend of the Shackleton kid."

"The police have the button," I said to Himmel. "It was given to them by the person I mentioned, the person who saw everything and finally came forward. That person saw you in the house, Mr. Himmel."

"What's going on?" Himmel asked McDermott. "You said — "

"Shut up!" McDermott said again.

"You were seen, Mr. Himmel," I said. "You were

seen by someone else who was in the house that day. And that person has finally told the police. They know."

"Oh, God," Himmel said. "Oh, God."

"Pull yourself together, Norm," McDermott said. "The only people in the house when it happened were Mary Shackleton, Harold and the baby, and the baby was tucked safely in his crib."

I think the reason it took so long for his words to register was that I had a lot of information to process — everything I had read about the day it happened, everything I had heard. And because I was still thinking it through, I said, "Jay wasn't a baby. He was two years old."

"Whatever," McDermott said. "He was too young to tell me, the social worker or anyone else what happened to his mother. And even if he could have told us anything, he would have had nothing to say. He wasn't anywhere near the basement when it happened."

Then, finally, my ankle throbbing, wondering if I was really hearing what I thought I was hearing or if I was just imagining it, I said, "And just exactly how do *you* know where Jay was?"

McDermott looked confused by the question. Himmel looked blank.

"When Linda Shackleton arrived at the house, Jay was in the basement with his mother," I said. "Everything I've ever heard or read about the case said Jay was traumatized because he saw his father murder his mother right before his eyes."

That wasn't how I saw it now, though. Now I saw

little Jay hearing a terrible noise down in the basement. I pictured him clamoring up and over the side of his crib the way Phoebe used to when she was old enough. I imagined him making his way down first one flight of stairs and then another, until he found his mother . . .

Dave McDermott looked even more confused, but Norman Himmel's eyes widened with understanding.

"I went down there to try to talk her out of giving the land to those environmentalists," Norman Himmel said slowly. "When she didn't answer, I went nuts. I thought I was too late to stop her. Then I saw the back door open, so I went in. I saw her lying at the bottom of the basement stairs. Then I saw something move down there. That's why I got out of there. Because I saw something move . . . But it wasn't Harold. It was *you*, wasn't it?" He was looking at McDermott as if he had just stumbled into the lair of a wild and vicious animal. "That's why you told me not to say anything about being there. *You* were there first."

"Norm, for the last time, *shut up!*" Dave McDermott said.

Norm didn't shut up, though. He said, "All that time I was afraid someone might have seen me in the house and think I had something to do with it, and it was *you*. You were the one — " He pulled a cell phone from his jacket.

Dave McDermott stared at it as if it were going to bite him. "What are you doing?"

"What I should have done five years ago. Tell the

police exactly where I was and what I was doing that day."

Dave McDermott's eyes turned hard and cold. "Are you going to tell them *everything*?"

I didn't know what he meant by that, but Norman Himmel seemed to. He stared down at his cell phone. He didn't punch in any numbers. Then they both looked at me.

Dave McDermott lunged toward me. I tried to duck him, but lost my balance and felt myself falling backwards. All I could think of were those big, hard, sharp-edged glacial deposits. That and how it would feel to land on them. Then I wasn't falling backwards anymore. Someone had me by the hand. Norman Himmel. He had caught me and was pulling me toward him. Then all my weight fell on my hurt ankle and I cried out.

Chapter 18

Pain makes it hard to concentrate. The thing I remember most about Norman Himmel helping me up from the trail that led down into the ravine was that I was trying as hard as I could not to cry. I saw Dave McDermott doubled up on the ground, but it didn't even occur to me to wonder how a car salesman could have managed to topple a former police officer. I saw a cell phone in Norman Himmel's hand, too, as I sat on the ground thinking that if I had a fairy godmother or if I were Aladdin with a lamp and three wishes, all I would ask for was painkillers, painkillers, painkillers.

The cavalry, in the form of Levesque and Steve Denby, with my mother and sister trailing behind, finally arrived. Steve and Norman Himmel carried me out of the park by doing one of the cross-your-arms-and-make-a-little-seat things. Levesque, I think, placed Dave McDermott under arrest. I didn't find out for sure until after my left ankle was encased in plaster. Mom was sitting in the emergency room with me, waiting for someone who had disappeared to find me a pair of crutches. Phoebe had gone to get me some juice. Then, suddenly, the curtain parted and there was Levesque.

"How are you feeling?" he said.

"It's broken this time."

He nodded. I knew what he meant by the spare

gesture — it could have been a lot worse.

"Did you arrest McDermott?"

For a moment I thought he was going to pull his official police business routine. But he didn't. Instead he pulled a plastic chair close to the bed, dropped down into it, and nodded.

"I thought it was Himmel," I said. "I was sure he had done it."

"So was I."

That surprised me. I hadn't thought he was taking me seriously.

"If I tell you what Norman Himmel said — "

"I promise not to tell a soul," I said. I put my hand over my heart and looked at my mother, who nodded in a solemn witness sort of way.

"You were right about Norman Himmel having no alibi," Levesque said. "It turns out that someone from the environmental group called him that morning to tell him that Mary Shackleton was going to sign her land over to them. He drove down to East Hastings to try to talk her out of it."

"That's why he wasn't at the Breakfast Club that morning and why he was late for his interview with Sally," I said.

Levesque nodded.

"He parked down the road and *walked* to Mary's."

"Why didn't he drive right up?"

"He was afraid that if she saw his car pull into the driveway, she would know it was him, and she wouldn't open the door."

"Which is why the neighbors didn't notice anything?"

He nodded.

"He knocked, but no one answered. Then he went around to the back and noticed that the door was ajar, so he knew someone had to be home. He went in, calling for her. He saw her lying at the bottom of the basement stairs. He says he saw something else move down there, but wasn't sure who or what it was."

I nodded. That was what Himmel had said in the park.

"So he took off?"

"He says all he could think was, if something had happened to Mary, maybe there was a chance to get the land after all. He left the house and drove back to Morrisville. Later, when he heard she was dead, he panicked. What if someone had seen him at the house? What if someone suspected him of being involved in her death? That's when he called McDermott, who told him to relax, that it was obvious Harold had done it. McDermott also told him to keep quiet about being in the house so that he didn't muddy the waters. Himmel agreed, but he couldn't stop worrying that someone had seen him."

"No wonder he reacted the way he did when I turned up asking questions five years later."

"That was one reason," Levesque said. "He had another, though."

I waited.

"You were right when you said Norman Himmel and his partners stood to make a lot of money on Mary Shackleton's land," Levesque said. "But you have to spend money to make money."

I'd heard that before, from Bob Chartoff. "All of them had invested money for planning and for an environmental assessment, right?" I said.

Levesque nodded. "Altogether, the partners in Toronto and the three up here invested well over a million dollars," he said. "Besides the planning and the assessment, they hired a consulting firm to put together a proposal and sell it to provincial and municipal officials and politicians. Apparently Norman Himmel was short of cash. He borrowed what he could from the bank, then he got the rest of what he needed from the car dealership where he worked."

"Got, as in, asked his boss for a loan?"

"Got, as in, didn't ask his boss for a loan."

"He stole the money?"

"The precise term is embezzlement," Levesque said.

That would explain why Norman Himmel threw me out of his office when I showed up asking questions.

"How do you know that?" I asked.

He looked at me long and hard before saying, "I told you I was going to look into it."

Yup. He did. And obviously he had.

"Himmel was counting on replacing the money he had taken without anyone catching on," he continued. "Then, when Mary's father died, the deal stalled and Himmel started to get nervous. He had to come up with some cash before he was caught. So he offered a piece of the action to his old friend — for a price."

"Dave McDermott was in on the deal?"

Levesque nodded. "As a silent partner. Himmel didn't want to have to explain to the others why he had let McDermott buy in — he didn't want anyone asking questions — so they agreed to keep it quiet. Two months before Mary Shackleton died, Dave McDermott took out a second mortgage on his house." He said this as if it meant something, but I wasn't sure what. "He took a loan using his house as collateral," Levesque explained. "He gave that money to Himmel, to replace what Himmel had embezzled. Which meant that the only way McDermott could get the money to pay off his bank loan was if the landfill deal went through. When it looked like it was going to be killed once and for all by Mary Shackleton, it didn't just mean that McDermott wasn't going to get rich, it also meant he wouldn't be able to pay back the bank. He was also in danger of losing everything he had."

"So Dave McDermott had a motive for murder too?"

Levesque nodded. "When he heard from Linda Shackleton that Mary was about to sign her land over to an environmental group, he went over to her house to stop her. When she refused to listen, he decided to take permanent action. Then, because he was in charge of the investigation, he didn't have much trouble laying the blame on Harold. Himmel complicated things a little, but not much. He was at the house, he saw Mary at the bottom of the stairs and did nothing about it, so it wasn't hard for McDermott to convince him to keep quiet to avoid Harold's lawyer suggesting that maybe someone else — Himmel, for example — had murdered Mary. That would have created reasonable doubt."

"Which might have meant Harold wouldn't get convicted and McDermott would have been forced to investigate more."

Levesque nodded. "It would also have drawn unwanted attention to Himmel," he said.

Something still bothered me, though.

"Why didn't Linda mention that Dave McDermott had been at her house when she got that phone call from Mary? Why did she keep quiet for him?"

"Because he had told her not to worry about Mary, even though he knew Harold had a bad temper. So after Harold supposedly killed Mary, he asked Linda not to say anything because he didn't want the whole world to know that he had exercised bad judgment. He told her he felt terrible about not taking her concerns seriously, and that maybe if he had listened to what she was saying, Mary would still be alive."

"And she believed him?"

"Why wouldn't she?" Levesque said. "She was in love with him. And, like everyone else, she had no reason to suspect McDermott. So far as anyone knew, he had no motive. There was nothing at all to link him to Mary."

My ankle was still throbbing, but somehow I felt content. Then I saw Levesque glance at my mother, and she got up and left. If that didn't signal trouble, I don't know what did.

"What you did was stupid," he said.

My cheeks burned. I had to choke back the sarcastic words, you're welcome.

"Confronting the two of them like that, they could have hurt you."

"They were *already* going to hurt me," I pointed out. "If I hadn't confronted them, you'd probably be scraping me up off the rocks on the floor of the ravine."

He looked evenly at me. "I'm glad you're okay," he said. "But when I say I'm looking into it, I'm looking into it, okay? No more mixing in police business. No more putting yourself in danger like that. Understood?"

This time I couldn't stop myself. This time I said it — "You're welcome."

* * *

"I can't believe it," Jonah said. He shook his head and looked a little dazed. "I've been dreaming about this day every day for the past five years, but now that it's here, I can't believe it." He had shown up on my doorstep first thing in the morning to tell me that he and Jay and his aunt were driving up to bring his father home today.

I couldn't believe it either. Or how fast things had moved after the day in the park. Dave McDermott had maintained his innocence, but then things started to pile up. Chief McDermott had known about Norman Himmel's embezzling, and not only had he done nothing about it, he had acted to help him cover it up. He had counseled Norman Him-

232

mel to lie about his whereabouts that day. He had tried to kill me to stop me from revealing his blunder about where Jay had been that morning. The button was matched to the ones on the uniform he had kept from his police days. He must have known that if he went to trial, his chances with a jury would not be good. Neither would his sentencing options. In the end, he agreed to plead guilty to second-degree murder in exchange for eligibility for parole after fifteen years.

"Believe it," I told Jonah as I balanced myself on my crutches. "Your dad is getting out of prison, and it's all because of you."

Jonah shook his head again. "It's because of *you*," he said. "You're the one who asked all those questions. You're the one who found the button. And you're the one who tripped up McDermott. It's all thanks to you, Chloe."

There was no way I could accept that. "You believed in your father when no one else did, Jonah," I said. "It was only because you were so determined that I got involved."

His face softened into a smile. It was a look I could definitely get used to.

"How about if we both take a little credit?" he said.

I laughed. "Fair enough," I said. "How's Jay? He must really be excited."

"He is," Jonah said. "I don't think any of us slept last night. We were all so keyed up that it was like a lifetime of Christmas Eves crammed into one night."

"Too bad that button didn't pop out of Mr. Edgar a whole lot earlier," I said.

Jonah's smile faded.

"I thought Jay was too young to remember Mom clearly," he said. "I made Aunt Linda put everything away so I wouldn't have to think about it, so I wouldn't have to remember. I didn't realize how much that hurt Jay. He hid that button so that I wouldn't find it. He thought I'd take it away from him if I did."

"You had no way of knowing that, Jonah," I said.

"I know. But if I hadn't underestimated Jay — "

"You didn't underestimate him. You just didn't know."

A car horn tooted at the end of the driveway. It was Linda Shackleton's car.

"Looks like it's time to go," I said.

Jonah waved at his aunt. Then he turned back to me and said, "I want you to meet my dad. You'll like him. I know he'll like you."

"I'd love to," I said.

He smiled again and, all of a sudden, he was kissing me on the cheek. Then he wasn't the only person smiling. I think I still had a goofy grin on my face long after he had bounded down the driveway, jumped into his aunt's car, and disappeared from sight.

Behind me, the front door opened. It was Levesque. I was still kind of angry with him. I had been responsible for Dave McDermott incriminating himself, but what had Levesque said? That what I had done was stupid. I had been told to stay

ut of police business and I had stuck my nose
mack into it. I was never, under any circum-
tances, ever to do anything like that again. Did I
nderstand that? Oh, yes, I did. And I was never,
nder any circumstances, ever to ask Levesque
nything about any investigation he was involved
1. Did I understand that? *Mais oui.* So when he
ame down the steps toward me I trembled a little,
nd not just from the cold. How ungrateful could a
erson be?

He had one of my sweaters in his hand, and held
out to me. "Your mother is convinced you're going
o catch pneumonia," he said. "You'd better put this
n."

I accepted it, but only because I was freezing.

"Jonah's on his way to bring his dad home," I
aid.

"I know," Levesque said. Then, "How about com-
ng inside and having some breakfast?"

I stood my ground.

"I'm making French toast. With real maple syrup.
ust the way you like it."

He had my attention.

"Quebec maple syrup?"

"Nothing but the best," he said, and I was almost
ure that I saw a little smile somewhere under that
oustache. "Think of it as a peace offering."

I smiled back and hobbled after him into the
ouse that had once belonged to Mary and Harold
hackleton.